L. BURKE

Odd man out

Anne was in Norfolk? Mom and Pop and Mickey and Anne were all together in Norfolk? My whole family was there—except me! I picked up my half-made tuna sandwich and hurled it across the room. I knocked over a kitchen chair and another one. I was closest to Mickey of anybody! Why wasn't I with them? I was eleven years old, dammit—not a baby, not a stupid idiot who couldn't visit a sick person!

Other Bullseye Books you will enjoy:

And the Other, Gold by Susan Wojciechowski
Beanpole by Barbara Park
Gaucho by Gloria Gonzalez
Toliver's Secret by Esther Wood Brady
Wild Iris Bloom by Mavis Jukes

Run, run, as fast as you can

BY

MARY

POPE

OSBORNE

Bullseye Books • Random House
New York

For my husband,
William Ronald Osborne

with special thanks
to Jean Marzollo and Amy Ehrlich

and in loving memory of T. D.

Prologue

When Pop first showed us a picture of our new house in Virginia, I whooped with joy. The house was white with green shutters, and sea grass, whipped by the wind, bordered the yard. The ocean was a stretch of blue beyond the grass. My brother Mickey and I thought this was going to be the best place we'd ever lived. I can still picture us laughing and clapping our hands. It's hard to believe that was only two years ago. Everything has changed so much since then.

1

I remember Mickey kept teasing me the day we moved from North Carolina to Virginia. I was sitting in the backseat of the car trying to concentrate on *Seventeen* magazine with Anne. But Mickey started barking in my face, pretending to be a dog.

"Stop it!" I yelled at him. "Mom, tell him to stop!"

Mom turned around and said, "Stop, baby."

But Mickey kept nuzzling me and slurping like a dog. I pushed his head away and tried not to laugh. "Don't," I said. "Mom!"

Mom reached back and put her hand on Mickey's back. "Sit up here, honey. Crawl over," she said.

Mickey threw one bare leg over the front seat. Then he heaved the rest of his skinny body over and crashed into Mom. For an eight-year-old, he was sort of a runt.

"Thank goodness," I said, and I settled back next to Anne. She turned a page of the magazine to some back-to-college fashions. "I like this," I said, pointing to a girl in a red terry-cloth V-neck top with no blouse underneath.

Anne smiled. "You're a little young for that," she said.

"I've seen lots of eleven-year-olds wear things like that!" I said.

"Okay, attention!" Pop said. "Look for signs to Holden Beach!"

I looked out the window. We were whizzing down a big boulevard, past Kentucky Fried Chicken and McDonald's. I felt like I always felt when we moved —like I was starting a whole new life. Our family had lived lots of places when Pop was in the Army. He'd retired last month and was going to work as a fund raiser for a junior college in Holden Beach.

We drove past Holden Elementary School. I turned and stared at the gray building. I pictured myself walking into the sixth grade wearing a red V neck like the one in the magazine. In North Carolina I'd been kind of childish. Here in Virginia I wanted to be mature and sexy like the girls in *Seventeen.*

Just then Mickey popped around and barked in my face. I barked back at him. Then I smacked his head and said, "Cut it out!" It was hard to act mature with him around.

"There, Bob," Mom said.

"Hup—here we go," Pop said. He turned off onto an exit and drove through a residential area.

"There's High Street," Mom said.

Pop turned right and drove toward the ocean. Tall grass was blowing at the end of the street. The sun had gone down, but the sky was still pink. Pop stopped the car in front of a white shingled house.

The smell of salt air hit us when we all piled out of the car. "Hallie, let's go!" Mickey yelled.

"Don't take off. Grab something and carry it in," Mom said.

We grabbed suitcases and boxes from the trunk of the car and carried them up to the house. Once we got inside, Pop gave us a tour. We surveyed the living room, kitchen, and dining room, then paraded up to the second floor.

"This is Mom's and my bedroom," Pop said as he led us through a door near the top of the stairs. "Mercy," Mickey said. His voice sounded hollow in the big empty room.

"That's the bathroom," Pop said, leading us back into the hall. "And that's Anne's room, and this big room is Mickey and Hallie's room." Pop pointed to the room opposite Anne's.

Damn! When would they realize I was too old to room with Mickey? When would they let me have my own room—or share a room with Anne! I yelled these things in my head, while on the outside I crossed my arms and stuck out my chin. But no one noticed me as they tramped into Anne's room like a bunch of goons. I stayed out in the hall and kicked the baseboard.

"Hallie, come!" Mom called. Pop stepped back into the hall.

"What's wrong, baby?" he asked me.

I'm not a baby, I thought. He and Mom always treated me like I was a baby.

"I want my own room," I said.

"We've only got three bedrooms," he said. Everybody came back out into the hall and stared at me.

My mouth trembled. "I'm too big to room with Mickey."

"But you always wanted to room with him before," Mom said.

I looked down at the floor and mumbled, "I know. But I want to be different here." Nobody said anything. I looked at Mom. "Maybe I can room with Anne."

"Well, you can take her room when she goes back to school," Mom said.

"No, now," I said. I wanted to start being different *now*.

"But you'll—" Mom said.

"I guess we can share a room," Anne broke in. "Then she can have it to herself when I leave."

"Can I, Mom?" I said.

"Well, if Anne doesn't mind. You two can take the big room."

"Oh, boy!" I said, and I scooted into the room to check it out. I looked out the window at the ocean. It was almost dark outside, but you could still see the whitecaps.

"Mickey, come look at the ocean!" I shouted. I felt a little bad for not wanting to share a room with him. When he came to the window, I leaned over and nuzzled his brown curly hair. He gently pushed my head away.

That night we all slept in sleeping bags on the living-room floor. Our furniture was coming the next day on the moving van. Lying in the dark, I could smell the new paint on the walls and hear the waves crashing against the beach. I felt great—we were living by the ocean; I was going to share a room with Anne; everything seemed fresh and new.

2

Mickey's feet woke me up early the next morning. He was poking me in the side with his toes and saying, "Hallie, Hallie." I opened my eyes. Mickey had already crawled out of his sleeping bag and was wearing his baggy tan shorts. "Let's explore," he whispered.

Everyone else was still sleeping. Pop was snoring. I crawled out of my bag and pulled on a pair of shorts and a T-shirt. In a couple of minutes we were out the door.

"Come on!" I shouted, and we took off, galloping barefoot over the sandy soil at the end of our street. Mickey ran beside me, slapping his butt with his right hand. He was pretending to be a cowboy whipping his horse.

We leaped over some dune grass and jumped from a little ridge onto clean white sand.

"Mercy," Mickey said, breathing hard. I thought this was a ridiculous thing for him to be saying all the time. He'd picked it up from his friend Tommy Barron, who lived near us in North Carolina. But the sight before us *was* amazing—a blue-green sea and a long beach; no people, not even a dog.

Suddenly Mickey jumped up and started screeching like a banshee. He could be so loud sometimes. I ran after him and we scared some gulls and ran to the edge of the ocean. We dared each other to step into the water. I was up to my calves, Mickey his knees, when I picked up a piece of wood coming in on a little wave. Suddenly I saw it was covered with some kind of tiny worms. A few of the worms even ran over my hand. I screamed and threw it from me, then galloped out of the water, still screaming.

Mickey didn't understand, but he started screeching and splashed after me. We ran like monsters were after us. Half playing and half serious, we ran over the sand, jumping over dead horseshoe crabs and hunks of seaweed. Finally we rested on some rocks.

"What's wrong? What'd you see?" Mickey said, gasping for breath.

"Worms," I said, shuddering. I wiggled my fingers and came toward him. "Worms! Worms!" I said.

Mickey screamed as I chased after him. His feet squeaked in the sand. He started saying in a silly voice, "Run, run, as fast as you can! You can't catch me, I'm the Gingerbread Man!" It made him seem like such a baby that I stopped running. But he kept taking little steps toward me, then jumping back. He said "worms" and wiggled his fingers, trying to get me to play.

"Don't, that's babyish. Look!" I said, pointing at the waves.

"What?" he said.

"Dolphins!"

"Mercy," Mickey said dramatically.

"Don't say that. It makes you sound like an old lady," I said.

"You're an old lady," he said.

"You're an old lady and a baby," I said.

Suddenly we heard Pop whistling for us. It was a special family whistle that we recognized anytime, anywhere. We ran back up to the dune grass together, shouting "Oww, oww, oww!" because the sand had gotten real hot and it was burning the heck out of our feet.

We saw the Mayflower van when we came over the ridge.

"Bosco!" Mickey shouted. Bosco was Mickey's stuffed bear who'd been traveling in the moving van with the rest of our things. "Get me out of this truck!" Mickey shouted in Bosco's voice. Bosco talked in a funny, deep voice.

"Shhh," I said

A moving man looked at us funny.

"Get me out!" Mickey said.

"Shut up, you nut!" I said. I pulled Mickey toward the house and pushed him through the doorway. He tripped and banged into one of the big boxes in the hall.

"Hey, attention!" Pop said as he was coming down the hall with Mom. Pop said lots of army things to me and Mickey, like "at ease," or "attention," or he called us "troops" sometimes and said it was time for inspection. He treated us like baby soldiers, I thought, because he didn't know how else to act. When he wasn't acting that way, he actually seemed sort of shy.

"Why'd you whistle for us?" I said.

"Because the van's here. I thought you'd want to watch them unload," Pop said.

"Can we get our bikes?"

"They'll bring them out, don't worry."

"What about Bosco?" Mickey said.

"They'll get him. Now, keep out of everyone's way."

"Go sit on the curb," Mom said.

We went back out and sat on the curb and watched the moving men.

Bosco came off the truck first. He was dusty and dead-looking. "Sit here," Mickey said, and he sat Bosco on the curb between us.

"Hello," someone said. We jerked around. A tall skinny woman with silver hair and a great tan was holding a hose and looking down at us. "Are you our new neighbors?" she said.

"Yes," I said.

"What are your names and ages?" She sounded like she was talking to people who couldn't speak English.

"Hallie Pine, eleven. And Mickey Pine—he's eight."

"Almost nine," Mickey said.

"Good. I'm Ruth Bankly. You'll have to meet my daughter. She's eleven too. Laney! Laney!"

A round face with glasses appeared at the front window of the house next door.

"Come meet our new neighbors, darling!"

Laney bounded out of her house. She ran like a big clumsy dog. She was breathing through her mouth and her glasses were falling down on her nose.

"Laney, this girl is your age. Her name is Hettie—"

"Hallie," I said.

"Sorry, dear, Hallie, and her brother—"

"Mickey," he said.

"That's right," Mrs. Bankly said. Of course it was right, I thought.

"Hi," Laney said, pushing her glasses back into place.

"Excuse me," Mrs. Bankly said, and she walked over and hosed her plants, leaving Laney standing there.

"What's that?" Laney said, pointing at Bosco.

"My brother's bear."

"What's he do?"

What's he do? He doesn't do anything, I thought —he's a stuffed animal. "Nothing," I said.

There was a pause for a second, then Laney said, "Where did you used to live?"

"North Carolina," I said. "But we just lived there two years. We've traveled all over the world— Florida, Oklahoma, Germany. My father was in the Army, but he just retired."

"My dad's in Texas," Laney said.

"On business?"

"No. He lives there; my parents are divorced."

"Oh." I didn't know what to say, so I looked back at the moving men.

"Do you have bikes?" Laney said.

"They're on the truck," Mickey said.

"Maybe we could ride around when they come off," Laney said.

"Good idea," Mickey said.

"Would you like me to show you the school this afternoon?" Laney said. I could tell she was talking to me. I turned back around.

"Yeah, I guess so," I didn't particularly want to play with her. I wanted to help Anne fix up our room. But I didn't know what else I could say.

"There's your bed," Mickey said.

We watched the men take my bed off the truck. Laney stood behind us, breathing loudly for a few minutes. Then she mumbled, "I'll see you later," and ran back to her house. I turned to say okay, but it was too late.

3

By noon a lot of boxes had accumulated upstairs. Anne and I got on our knees in our room and started unpacking them. From the boxes marked HALLIE I dragged out a bunch of toys and dolls. I called Mickey to come upstairs.

"You want this?" I said, holding up a stuffed monkey.

"What's wrong with it?" he said.

"Nothing. I've just outgrown it."

Anne giggled.

"I *have* outgrown it! You want it?" I said, holding the monkey out to her.

"No, thanks," she said.

"I want it," said Mickey. "What else?"

I gave him all my stuffed animals, except a little lamb Anne had given me the year before. I gave him my dollhouse—he said he wanted it for his army men. He took my Betty Crocker cooking kit and a bunch of children's books and my Barbie doll furniture. He didn't want Barbie. I really didn't want to give her up anyway. When Mickey and Anne were out of the room, I stuck Barbie and Ken and Midge in the back of my bottom dresser drawer. Just as I was covering them with a doll blanket, Laney, the girl from next door, appeared in the doorway. I jumped.

"Your mom told me to come up," she said, pushing her glasses back into place.

"Oh, hi," I said as I quickly closed my drawer.

"You want to ride bikes now? I saw yours out on the grass."

I stood up and dusted off my knees. "Well, I guess for a little while. Then I have to help my sister fix up our room," I said.

"Is that your Cover Girl stuff?" Laney asked, pointing to Anne's open makeup kit on the windowsill.

"No, it's my sister's," I said. Laney sure is nosy, I thought.

I followed Laney on my bike down Water Street till we came to the elementary school. It was a pretty big school, compared to some of the schools I'd known. Next to it was a junior high for seventh, eighth, and ninth graders.

I was starting to feel pretty excited by the time we parked our bikes and walked over to peer through the windows at the empty classrooms.

"The sixth-grade classes are down there," Laney said.

"Oh, they are?" I was trying to sound nonchalant, but my heart was pounding. I felt like it wouldn't be long—just a few weeks before I'd be an important person around here. I'd been president of my class in North Carolina. Just about my whole life I'd been president or vice-president of my class. And last year I'd had the lead in the school play and I was head of the safety patrols.

"Follow me this way," Laney said. Just as she said that, she tripped and fell down. She giggled and pushed her glasses back into place and got up. I couldn't help thinking Laney was kind of a chump. I figured she'd be the kind of friend I played with around the house, but not in school. In my old school, I'd always hung out with the most popular kids.

Laney led the way around the corner of the building. Then she stopped and said, "That's the football team for the junior high. They're called the Red Devils. See—way out there—" She pointed at some little figures in the distance doing jumping jacks "They're practicing for the fall."

"Can a sixth grader be a cheerleader?" I asked

"No, just junior-high girls."

Damn, well, that was something I'd have to wait and do next year, I thought.

Laney and I rode home. I think she wanted me to invite her in, but I told her I had to help Anne fix up our room and I'd see her later. As I was parking my bike Mom was going into the house carrying a bag of groceries. She stopped and said, "Hallie, where were you? Mickey was looking all over for you."

"Oh, he expects to do everything with me."

"He really wanted to go with you," she said.

"Where is he?" I sighed.

The next morning while we were eating breakfast, Laney knocked at the front door. Mom let her in and I heard them talking in the hall. Laney asked Mom if I could go to the municipal pool. Mom said, "Oh, yes, she'd love to."

"Damn," I whispered angrily.

"You'll have fun," Anne said softly.

"Can I go?" Mickey said.

I nodded and dragged myself up from the break-fast table. I went upstairs and changed into my bathing suit, then joined Mickey and Laney outside.

The pool was noisy and crowded when we got there. We parked our bikes next to an aluminum fence and paid fifty cents at the gate. We dropped our stuff on the grass inside and ran and jumped into the water.

We swam for a while, then the three of us crawled out of the water and sat on our towels looking like three wet chickens—especially me and Mick, because our curly hair shrunk up real close to our heads when it was wet.

"See that table of kids over there?" Laney said, pointing. "Those are the most popular girls I know. They're the stars." A group of kids was sitting around a table with a transistor radio blaring away. The girls wore tight bathing suits. They had pretty good figures.

"Hi, Jeanie!" Laney called to one of the girls in the group. The girl looked around and then looked back at the others. She shrugged like she didn't know who Laney was. It was sort of embarrassing.

"Her mother's a friend of my mother's," Laney said casually, pushing her glasses back in place. I stared at Jeanie. She wore a baby-blue bikini kind of suit and was combing out her long blond hair.

"Jeanie goes with Jack Thomas even though she's a sixth grader and he's a seventh grader," Laney said.

"*She's* a sixth grader?" I said.

"Yeah, all those girls are sixth graders."

I couldn't believe it. None of my friends in North Carolina looked like this. Suddenly I felt creepy, wearing my plaid bathing suit with the little skirt, sitting there all scrunched up and shivering.

"You want a Popsicle?" Mickey said, jumping up.

I shook my head. He grabbed his blue sailor hat and ran pigeon-toed to the concession stand.

"Jack's a great football player," Laney said. I shrugged and made a face like "big deal," but I couldn't help looking at Jack and Jeanie. She was talking to him flirtatiously, pointing her comb at him. She was tanned and her silky blond hair sparkled. I studied the other girls. A Coke can glinted in the sun as one of them lifted it to her mouth. She was tanned, too, with long straight brown hair.

I stared at the group until Mickey came back, licking his orange Popsicle. His lips were orange and so was his tongue. "Want some?" he asked, smiling at me. His front teeth were orange too. He looked ridiculous standing there so skinny in his baggy bathing suit. His sailor hat was way too big for his head. I glanced at Laney. She looked goofy, too, sort of fat and plain. Suddenly I felt embarrassed to be seen with the two of them. I didn't want those popular kids to see us.

"Let's go!" I said, jumping up.

The two of them followed me out to the bike rack.

All the way home I hashed over what I'd just seen. What could I do to look more mature, I wondered—maybe if I could change my hairstyle and get some new clothes . . . But what could I do about my skinny body? For the first time I began to worry about what my status in this new school would be.

4

On Saturday Anne went back to college. She was a sophomore at the University of North Carolina. The morning she left, we were alone in our room packing her suitcases. I was running my hand over her new towels. I loved them. They were yellow and blue checkered.

"While I'm gone, you can play my records if you want," she said.

"I can?"

"My old ones."

"Like what?"

"Like these," she said, stooping by her record shelf. Her brown wavy hair fell over her shoulders as she ran her fingers over the ends of some record jackets. "Judy Collins," she said, "Bob Dylan, Dolly Parton . . . all the records at this end from here over."

"Thanks!" I said. "Do you like my hair this way?"

"What's different?"

"My barrettes!"

"Oh, I couldn't see them."

She was right. My hair was a bush of white curls; you couldn't even see the two tortoiseshell barrettes I'd bought at Woolworth's the day before.

"I wish my hair was long and straight," I said.

"Your hair's real cute."

We were quiet for a second. "How old were you when you started wearing a bra?" I said.

"I'm not sure."

Not sure! But her breasts were so big, she'd probably never had to worry. We sure weren't alike in that way. I was a board—that's what Tommy Barron, that kid in North Carolina, had said. Mickey told me Tommy said I was a board. Mickey didn't know what that meant, but I did.

"Are you worried about your chest developing?" Anne said.

Tears filled my eyes. I was thinking about Tommy Barron and those girls at the pool and realizing Anne was going away and I wouldn't have anyone I could really talk to. My mother didn't talk to me like Anne did. Mom called me dolly and baby; she treated me like I was Mickey's age.

"There are junior bras you can get," Anne said.

"There are?"

"Sure. I think you can even get one with a little padding in it to make it look like you have something." I pushed my tongue against my cheek to keep from crying, and I nodded.

"Ready, Annie?" Pop called from downstairs. "Let's load the car." Damn, I thought, there was so much I wanted to ask her about, but I couldn't even think of what to say next.

Anne snapped her suitcases shut. Pop appeared in the doorway.

"Let's move the troops out!" he said, clapping his hands together. Pop was smiling, but I knew he was just pretending to be cheerful. It made me mad sometimes when he acted fakey like that.

Anne took two bags, Pop carried two bags, and I picked up one. I stumbled behind them, panicked, trying to think up some more questions. I was so mad at myself—why had I waited until the last minute to ask her things?

"Do you like velour?" I said as we banged down the stairs.

"What?"

"Do you like velour?"

"Sure," she said.

"Me too."

"Have you got everything, darling?" Mom said at the bottom of the stairs. Pop was driving Anne to Chapel Hill and Mom was staying with me and Mickey.

"Come, baby, your sister's leaving," Mom called to Mickey. He was watching cartoons.

All of us went out to the car and helped load it. I felt terrible. Anne kissed Mom and Mickey. She touched my hair and said, "Really, I think your curls are wonderful."

When the car pulled away, tears were running down my cheeks.

"She's crying," Mickey said to Mom, pointing at me.

"Leave her alone," Mom said.

5

I felt a little better about my looks after talking to Anne. I thought if she liked my hair, it couldn't be that bad. And I asked Mom to take me to shop for some new clothes. I wanted to get a red top like the one I'd seen in *Seventeen* and a bra with a little padding in it.

A couple of days before school started, we went to the shopping center. I was nervous in the car, wondering how I should ask Mom about the bra. Finally I said, "Mom, I need some underwear." She said, "Okay."

When we got to Penney's, I headed for the girls' underwear section. Mom stopped to look at some purses. "Go pick out what you need," she said. "I'll be over in a minute."

I scooted to the girls' bras. I didn't see any padded ones, so I grabbed a regular kind, size 28AA, and carried it into a dressing room. It didn't fit; it was too tight across my back. I charged back out and grabbed a 30A. I tried it on, but it was too big in the cups—the material caved in where my breasts should have been.

"Hallie," Mom called.

"Just a minute."

"What are you doing?"

"Wait!" I said, scrambling to unhook the bra.

Suddenly she pulled back the curtain. I covered myself and yelped, "Don't!"

"What in the world?" she said.

"Go away!" I said. She closed the curtain; I got out of the bra and put my T-shirt back on. I was so damn embarrassed. She didn't have to say "What in the world?" so loud.

I came out of the dressing room. Before I could say anything, Mom looked at me with a little smile and said, "What on earth were you doing?"

"I was trying this on," I whispered angrily.

"What for? You don't need that yet."

I hated her for saying that. I put the bra down and flounced away from her, not even trying to make a case for myself. She just wouldn't understand what it meant to me.

She caught up with me in the sweater section. "What else can we get you?" she said, trying to be nice.

"I want a red terry-cloth V neck," I said coldly.

Mom and I looked in a bunch of stores. We couldn't find one. Mom wanted to leave, but I was determined. I thought if I couldn't get a bra, at least I should get the right top.

"Well, let's check in Sears," Mom said.

I didn't expect Sears to have it. But they did have something similar—a red V-neck velour top. I tried it on. I liked it because it sort of bloused out in front, making it look like I had a figure. I went out to show Mom.

"You'll burn up in that," she said.

"No, I won't," I said. "Let's get it. Anne likes velour."

"I like it, too, but not in summer."

"Well, I definitely want it," I said.

Mom shook her head doubtfully, but she let me buy it.

As soon as we got home, I closed my door and put on my velour top and a blue skirt and my red sneakers. I put my tortoiseshell barrettes in my hair and put on a Dolly Parton record. I looked in the mirror; this was what I was going to wear the first day of school. I felt excited, staring at my new outfit, having Anne's room all to myself, listening to Dolly sing this sexy song, "Here You Come Again." Satisfied, I took off my new outfit and spread it out on the bed. I really wanted to show it off to someone. I called Laney and told her to come over.

Laney came over and admired everything. I was getting a little worried about her, though. She was planning for us to ride our bikes to school together every day, and she was upset because we'd been assigned to different sixth grade classes. She wondered how we could arrange to have that changed.

"I don't know," I said. "I think we'll just have to take the class that's been assigned to us." I was glad we were going to be in different classes. I wanted to be a part of that group of kids I saw at the pool, and Laney definitely didn't seem to fit in with them.

The day after we looked at my new outfit, Laney called me to come over and look at her new outfit. Laney's house was dirty, as usual; it smelled like cigarette smoke. Her mother seemed so disorganized. I'd heard my mother say to Anne that she thought Mrs. Bankly might have a drinking problem.

"See—" Laney said when we got to her room. She'd laid her outfit out on the bed. It was a denim skirt and a long-sleeved red jersey! She thought it was neat that our outfits were so similar. I thought it was disgusting. I tried to think up an excuse for not riding to school with her the next day.

After a while I got up to go. I said, "Oh, I have to

go with Mickey to school tomorrow. It's a family tradition. I take care of him the first day, help him get situated and everything, you know. It's a drag. But I guess you and I can't ride together." I didn't look at her. There wasn't much logic in my excuse— why couldn't she just ride with both of us? But I didn't wait for her to suggest that. I said good-bye and got out of her house as fast as I could.

6

When I came down the stairs the next morning in my new outfit, Pop was walking through the hall on his way to work. He looked up at me.

"How do I look?" I said.

"Oh, you look sharp," he said.

"You like my outfit?"

"I think it's real sharp," he said. I laughed and said "sharp" was a funny word. Pop laughed too.

Mickey and Mom were in the kitchen discussing French toast.

"I suppose it did come from France," Mom was saying. "Honey, don't pour on so much syrup!"

"I don't want much," I said to Mom as I walked into the room. She was standing at the counter, putting food on my plate. I sat down, my stomach churning.

"You've got to eat something," she said. "You look sweet." She put my French toast in front of me. "Aren't you supposed to wear a blouse underneath a top like that?"

"No!" I said.

"Okay, okay." She held up her hands. "It looks great."

"Are you nervous?" Mickey said.

"Why should I be?" I said defensively.

"I'm nervous," he said. "I hope my teacher's nice."

I shrugged. It wasn't the teacher that worried me. I was thinking about the kids in my new class. I wished I could just leap over this "new girl" phase and settle into a popular place—be president of the class, make some neat friends, get a boyfriend, and get on with life.

I picked at my French toast until Mom finally said, "I can see you're not going to eat that. You two better get going."

Just before I left the kitchen, I turned to her and said, "How do you think my hair looks?"

"Baby, it looks beautiful," she said.

Mickey and I rode our bikes to Holden Elementary and parked at the bike stand.

"What's your room number?" I said.

Mickey pulled out a little slip of paper from his breast pocket. He was wearing a white short-sleeved shirt and blue pants. For a second, I wished I was him. He seemed so carefree in his clean little outfit.

"Three thirty-nine," he said.

"Okay, let's go," I said. I put my hand on his back and steered him toward the building. I escorted him to the door of room 339. We peeked in the doorway together. There was a tremendously fat woman sitting at the teacher's desk. Mickey looked quickly at me and said, "That's okay." I think he was afraid I'd tease him.

"I know," I said.

He said good-bye to me, then he went on in. His teacher gave him a friendly smile.

On the way to my classroom I decided to duck in the girls' room and rework my barrettes. I wanted to put them a little higher in my hair.

I fanned myself as I stared in the mirror. I thought I looked pretty good. I was hot, but I loved my red velour top.

The door to the girls' room opened.

"Oh, stop, you two!" It was that blond girl, Jeanie, with two other girls I'd seen at the pool. They were laughing. They seemed sort of windblown and rosy-cheeked.

"Give me your comb," Jeanie said to one of the girls.

"No." The girl laughed.

"Give me yours," Jeanie said to the other girl.

"No!" They were teasing her.

"You creeps. Give me yours," she said, turning suddenly to me.

I handed her my comb.

"Oh, thanks!" she said, laughing at the other girls, like "so there!" Then she stood in front of the mirror and combed her long blond hair. I didn't know what to do while she combed. I didn't want to stare at her. So I just crossed my arms and looked at the sink. The three of them were giggling and shoving each other while they fixed their hair.

Finally Jeanie finished. She took her time pulling out her hairs from my comb, then handed it back without looking at me and said, "Thanks a lot." The three of them left, laughing all the way out.

The bathroom was quiet. I looked in the mirror. I looked like an immature idiot—frizzy hair and skinny shoulders. I was so hot in my new velour top, I could hardly stand it.

My status in this new school was definitely not going to be what it had been in North Carolina.

Our class held elections the first week and of course I didn't get voted into any office—not even nominated—because nobody knew me. On Army posts it had never mattered if I was new, because almost everybody was new. But here kids seemed to have known each other for years. It amazed me later to think that I'd expected to be popular right off the bat.

Two smart guys were elected class president and vice-president. They were well-known for their intelligence, apparently, but not for their looks or personalities. The kids in my class who were popular because of their looks and personalities were Jeanie and Paula and Stephanie—those three girls who were at the pool and in the bathroom. Laney was right— they were the stars.

The first few weeks of school the three of them hardly noticed me, even though I sat in the back of the room next to them. But I studied them and listened to everything they said. Gradually I got up the courage to make some funny comments to them. The first time they really appreciated me was one Friday afternoon during art period. We were all watercoloring pictures of blowfish and I cracked them up with a joke.

"Hallie Pine, do you want to tell the whole class what you said that was so funny?" said Mr. Edge, our teacher.

"No, sir," I said, my face getting red. What I'd said was my blowfish looked a lot like Miss Klinger, Mickey's fat teacher.

"Do your work then without talking," Mr. Edge said. But he gave me a look like he'd heard what I'd said about Miss Klinger. It made me feel guilty. I tried to keep my mouth shut for the rest of art period, but it was hard because I liked making those girls laugh.

After the bell I loitered near my desk, hoping to walk out with Jeanie and Paula. But suddenly Mickey popped his head in my class. He started making goofy expressions at me. Damn, I thought, any minute he'll talk like Bosco Bear. I waved him to go on, but he kept standing by the door, crossing his eyes. I grabbed my things and hurried over to him.

"You should wait for me at the bike stand," I said, and I rushed down the hall ahead of him.

On the way home Mickey called from his bike, "Hallie, could you be monitor for my Cub Scout badges?"

"What's that mean?"

"You mark down things I do, like tying knots."

"I guess so."

"Neil Larsen's going to work on his badges with me."

"Who's Neil Larsen?"

"He's in my den. He's neat."

"Why's he neat?"

"He's real funny. He has all these pet turtles. He acts like they're people."

"Pretty weird," I said. That sounded like Jeanie, I thought. "Pretty weird," I said again.

7

The next day was Saturday. It was a custom on Saturdays for Pop to take me and Mickey on little excursions, like to an open field to play catch or to a movie. This Saturday Pop wanted to take us to his new office at Methodist College, where he worked.

I had a tap class on Saturday morning—I'd been taking tap for several years—and after class I ran out to the parking lot to meet Mickey and Pop. I was in a good mood. We'd been learning a Hawaiian dance and I thought I could really do it well. I tossed my grass skirt and tap shoes on the backseat of the car and climbed in. We drove to the college.

Mickey and I swiveled in Pop's office chair; we met the janitor; then we went to the snack bar for burgers.

"Jesse, I'd like you to meet my daughter, Hallie, and my son, Mickey," Pop said to the guy serving burgers behind the counter. Pop was always friendly to people who waited on him. But I don't think Jesse even knew who Pop was.

After we ate our burgers, we walked around the school grounds. The wind was blowing leaves across the grass. The air was sunny and crisp. Two pretty teen-age girls—one in a blue blazer and one in a snowy gray turtleneck sweater—passed by us. They were talking and laughing, their hair blowing in the breeze.

Suddenly I felt a little wild, like I didn't want to be with Mickey and Pop. I wanted to be somewhere with the popular kids, like watching a football game or hanging out at the shopping center.

"Maybe we should go now," I said.

"You babies want Dairy Queens?" Pop said.

"Yeah!" Mickey exclaimed.

"We're not babies!" I said.

"Oh, excuse me," Pop said jokingly. But his face got a little red.

When we got to the parking lot, Pop started to take hold of our hands, but I pulled away and ran ahead of him and Mickey, thinking I was eleven, not eight. When we got in the car, I sat in the front seat. I felt a little bad about pulling away from Pop, so I leaned over and rubbed his "old gray head," as he called it. He took my hand and kissed it.

"Hallie, you want chocolate or vanilla?" Mickey said, resting his chin on the back of my seat.

"I really don't care," I said, turning to look out the window.

We drove to Ocean Boulevard. We stopped at a red light and I glanced over at McDonald's. Just as I'd imagined—a group of kids was sitting under one of those big metal umbrellas, eating and drinking. I saw Paula and Stephanie. I figured Jeanie was there too, and they'd all just come from a football game. My heart ached. I *was* a baby compared to them.

We pulled into the Dairy Queen parking lot. "I'll get the treats," Pop said.

Mickey jumped out with him. I let my arm dangle out the window and drummed my fingers against the side of the car. Suddenly I was mad at Mickey and Pop.

"Here, Hal, it's vanilla," Mickey exclaimed, handing me a cone through the window. He climbed back into the car. I didn't say anything. I licked my ice cream slowly, trying to have some dignity.

We were halfway home when Mickey said, "My stomach hurts."

I looked back at him. He was holding his cone out to the side, letting the ice cream drip over his fingers and onto the car seat.

"Pop, he's spilling ice cream everywhere!" I said.

Pop glanced over his shoulder. "What's the trouble, bud?"

"My stomach hurts."

"Well, don't spill your cone everywhere!" I said.

When we got home, Pop told Mom that the burgers at the snack bar had upset Mickey's stomach. Mom made Mickey lie down on the couch in front of *Wide World of Sports*. She kissed him and covered him with an afghan. He fell asleep.

"Hallie, if you're going to practice tap," my mother said, "please close your door so you don't wake him up."

"I'm not going to tap," I said. Tapping seemed dumb to me then. I felt like an idiot, picturing myself in my grass skirt, waving my arms and tapping my brains out. I grabbed the transistor radio from the sideboard in the kitchen and slipped out the front door.

The sun was setting, streaking the sky with pink. I sat huddled on our porch steps listening to a rock station. I imagined that Jeanie or Paula had just called to ask me to go to a football game with them. I tried to picture a good outfit to wear. I finally decided on a snowy gray turtleneck sweater.

It was almost dark when I spied Laney coming up our street. She was standing on her bike pedals, head down, heaving from side to side. I grabbed my radio and hurried back into the house.

Mickey stirred on the couch when I walked into the living room.

"How's your stomachache, baby?" Mom asked him.

"It's gone," he said.

8

Jeanie and Paula and Stephanie didn't ride bikes to school. They walked. Jack, Jeanie's seventh-grade boyfriend, walked with them. At about eight o'clock every day I'd see them out the kitchen window while I ate my cereal. They'd be crossing the intersection of our street and Water Street.

On the Monday after I saw the kids at McDonald's, I asked Mom to wake me up early. I finished my breakfast by ten till eight and was combing my hair in the hall mirror when Mickey came down the stairs.

"I'm walking today, squirt blossom," I said. My voice shook a little. I was nervous.

From the stairs Mickey reached out with his fist and bonked my head.

"Cut it out!" I said angrily.

He looked surprised, then he mimicked me. "Cut it out!"

"Oh, drop dead," I said.

"Dolly, don't be so ugly," Mom called from the kitchen.

"I'm not ugly! He's ugly! He hit my hair!"

"Don't yell."

"I'm not yelling! You always take his side!"

I picked up my notebook and stormed out of the house. When I got to the front steps, I stopped. Should I wait for the kids here, I wondered, or start walking slowly?

I started walking slowly, very very slowly. I guess I looked like a fool, but I didn't want to get to the intersection too soon.

Suddenly I saw them—Jeanie and Paula and Jack crossing my street. Jack had his books tucked under his arm like they were a football. Jeanie's long blond hair was blowing behind her. She wore a bright red sweater.

I walked forward, my knees feeling weak. On Water Street I fell in about fifty feet behind them and kept that distance all the way to school. Once Paula turned and saw me. She waved, but then she turned back around and kept yakking to Jack and Jeanie. I thought, That's okay—if I do this every morning, the day's bound to come when we all walk together.

My new plan excited me so much, it helped me be especially funny in class that day.

At one point Jeanie said, "Hallie, can I borrow some paper?"

"Yes-you-may," I said with an accent like an Indian from India.

Jeanie cracked up. "Do that for Steph," she said. "Steph, listen to Hallie. May I borrow some paper?"

"Yes-you-may," I said again like an Indian. I knew how Indians talked because an Indian family had lived next door to my family in North Carolina.

"Why-are-you-laughing?" I said in that funny voice. "What-is-so-funny?"

"She's a riot," Jeanie said, meaning me.

"What-is-so-funny?" I said.

"Hallie Pine—stop talking!" Mr. Edge said.

I nodded quickly and looked down at my book, but I felt delighted.

Jeanie was ahead of me in the lunch line that day. After she paid, she paused and waited for me to pay.

"Over there," she said casually, nodding her head toward some seats. We sat down and saved places for Paula and Steph.

I was so nervous, I couldn't eat my meat loaf, so I spent most of my time talking like an Indian to make them laugh. At one point I got carried away and started acting dumb. I bonked myself on the head like an eight-year-old. But I quickly turned even that into a good joke. I rattled away as an Indian, then I bonked myself and talked normal again. The girls thought I was a riot.

"Hi, Hallie." I looked up. Laney was crossing the lunchroom toward her class's tables and grinning at me. She seemed impressed that I was sitting with these girls. I nodded slightly to her, and she kept walking.

"Who-was-that-large-girl?" I said like an Indian. Jeanie choked and nearly spewed her milk across the table.

Steph slapped Jeanie on the back. I was feeling a little hysterical.

After school I loitered near my desk, but the three of them didn't notice me as they packed up their books and bustled out of the classroom. I followed them. From the steps I watched them all pile into Jeanie's mother's car. She's probably taking them to the mall to shop for clothes, I thought.

I walked on home. At one point, Mickey and Neil Larsen passed me on their bikes.

"There she is!" Neil shouted.

"Enemy alien!" Mickey shouted. "Shoot!"

They shot me and drove on.

I knew they were just trying to be funny, but it made me mad. "Grow up!" I shouted at their backs.

9

I ate lunch with Jeanie, Paula, and Steph every day after that. But I still didn't walk to school with them. Or go to football games with them or go to McDonald's with them. I was their friend in school, but not out of school. I thought boys might have something to do with this. Out of school these girls all hung around with seventh-grade boys. I guess they thought I wasn't mature enough for that.

But I was desperate to be with that group. Every morning I waited on our porch for them to get to the intersection. Then I charged forward, slowing down as I got closer to them. They saw me most days. The girls waved, but they never shouted, "Hallie, come join us."

I blamed it on my curly hair and my lack of breasts and my skinny legs. And I decided that I walked and laughed funny.

One gray Saturday in November I tried to change my walk and my laugh. All morning I walked up and down our street, taking little steps and swinging my arms. At the same time I practiced laughing without moving my face much. I made little chuckling sounds like "heh-heh-heh."

"Pretty weird," Mickey said later when we were watching cartoons and I was laughing this way.

"Shut up. You're weird," I said, and I composed myself to laugh again.

"Neil's coming over. Can you monitor our Scout badges?"

"Get Bosco to be your monitor," I said sarcastically. Bosco was sitting on the couch between us.

"Who me? Me?" Mickey shouted in Bosco's voice. "I'm not a monitor!"

"You're a baby with that thing," I said.

"You're a baby!" he said, half like Bosco and half like himself.

"See—you're even acting like a baby now," I said, "copying everything I say!"

"Ah, get out of here."

"You get out of here. You're a little baby. Kuchi-kuchi-coo," I said, poking him a little under his chin.

"Don't," he said, pushing my hand away.

"Kuchi-kuchi-coo."

"Watch it," he said. Then he talked like Bosco. "I'm not a baby!" he said. He held Bosco up in front of me. "I'm a mature bear!" He shoved Bosco in my face. He was laughing.

"Damn you! You drive me crazy!" I shouted, and I pushed Mickey real hard. He crashed against the coffee table and fell onto the floor.

Mickey looked stunned, then he burst out crying. I could hear him sobbing as I banged out the front door.

I yanked my bike out of the garage and got on. I drove straight to the shopping center. By now I could practically sniff out that group of popular kids.

I parked my bike on the sidewalk and stalked into the mall. Sure enough, there they were by Taco Takeout: Paula and Jeanie and Stephanie and Jack and two guys I didn't know, drinking Cokes. My heart was pounding like crazy, but I walked my new way of walking up to the counter, taking little steps, holding my arms straight and swinging them back and forth.

"Hi, Hallie," Paula said. I nodded casually and smiled. I ordered a Coke and a taco, then walked over and stood with the group. I was mad at myself for getting a taco. No way could I eat it and keep my dignity.

At first I just held the taco and took little sips of Coke. I watched the group intently. I didn't say anything, but occasionally I went "heh-heh-heh" at their remarks. Then grease from my taco began soaking through the waxed paper, gumming up my hand. I grew afraid to look at the taco for fear of drawing attention to it. The taco started feeling heavier and heavier. I got so scared that after a couple of minutes I couldn't move my hands or turn my head. My *heh-heh-heh*'s stuck in my throat. I stopped blinking. My brain was in a frenzy.

Suddenly Jack said, "Let's go to the Record Shack!" I felt terrified, but I moved my elbows and took a deep breath. I turned and dumped the taco into a garbage can. My hand was wet and greasy. I ran over to the counter and grabbed some napkins. By the time I'd wiped off my fingers, the group was walking off. Quickly I walked my new way of walking after them.

Jeanie and Jack were walking together. Jeanie was laughing. "Oh, that's cruel," I heard her say. They started walking faster. What's so important at the Record Shack? I wondered. I quickened my short steps. The whole group now was walking faster and faster. Suddenly Jack said, "Go!" and everybody took off running. I started running after them. They nearly knocked over some shoppers as they ran down the concourse; a couple of them looked back at me and giggled. It took a second before I realized what was happening: They were running from me.

I stopped. A scarlet feeling spread over my face. Then I turned and walked out of the mall to my bike.

I cried all the way to our house. When I parked my bike, I reached into my coat pocket and took out my sunglasses and put them on.

I walked up our front steps, opened the door, and peered in. Mom was dusting in the hall.

"Oh, hi," I said.

"Hallie, you really upset Mickey this morning!"

"Where is he?"

"He's on the beach with Neil. Now, be—"

I closed the door and walked off the porch. I started walking down our street. When I got to the sea grass, I walked faster. When I hit the sandy ridge, I took off running as hard as I could, running from those kids like they had run from me.

10

I ran down to the water. The wind over the sand was cold and damp. Sea gulls were swooping in the gray air. When I got to the edge of the water, I stopped and gasped for breath. I took off my sunglasses, then I crossed my arms and jumped up and down, trying to shake off my thoughts. I saw Mickey and Neil down the beach playing by the dunes. I took off running toward them. I slowed down halfway and walked quickly, wondering what to say to Mickey. Should I tell him I was sorry for pushing him? I decided no, I'd just act friendly and play with him, behave like nothing had happened. I started running again. "Hey!" I shouted.

Neil looked at me and waved. Mickey didn't look at me—not even when I got to them.

"Hi, Hal," Neil said. He was smiling and he gave me a little salute. Neil was a character. I'd heard Mom say he was a "gifted child."

Mickey tugged the back of Neil's coat and said, "Let's go up to our fort."

"Oh, where's your fort?" I said in a friendly way.

"It's—" said Neil.

"Don't tell her!" said Mickey.

"Why not?" said Neil.

"Just don't. Come on," Mickey said. He picked up a stick and started climbing like a mountain climber.

Damn, this was all I needed! I could tell he was paying me back for being mean to him that morning. "Why can't I come?" I said.

"Just don't!" Mickey shouted.

"Mickey! Why can't I come up!" My voice grew shrill.

"Go away!"

"Why?" I screamed.

He didn't answer. "I'm coming anyway," I shouted. I walked over to the dune and started climbing up after Neil.

"Hallie, get down!" Mickey shouted from the top of the dune.

I was pulling myself up by handfuls of dune weeds.

"Let her come," Neil said.

"No! Hallie, get down!" Mickey threw his stick at me, but it missed.

"Please let me," I said, looking up at him.

"No!" he said.

"Please."

He threw a dirt clod at me. I ducked and slipped, but grabbed a clumpful of grass to stop myself. "Please, can I come up?"

"Why—so you can wreck everything?"

"I want to play."

"Play?" he said scornfully.

"Yes, play."

"No! Get down!" Mickey shouted and he kicked some sand that avalanched down on me.

"Mickey, don't!" I screamed. I got sand in my hair and my eyes. I was trembling with my eyes closed, clinging to the weeds. I couldn't stand it that he wouldn't let me play with them. There was silence for a minute except for the whitecaps crashing against the beach.

"Mickey," I said, "I won't wreck anything."

He didn't say anything.

"Mickey . . ."

"Oh, okay," he said.

I climbed on up to the top. The three of us didn't say anything for a while as we stared at the waves. It was cold and the wind was blowing.

"Look—dolphins," Mickey said. About three or four of them were rolling up and down through the rough water.

"Hey, boys!" Neil shouted, and he whistled.

"You calling them in?" Mickey said.

"Yeah, the leader's mine!" Neil said.

"What for?" said Mickey.

"To ride," said Neil. "That stray one's Hallie's." He pointed to one that was a little off from the others.

"Where's mine?" Mickey asked, making a face.

"There!" Neil said. He pointed to one that had just surfaced. I don't know if it was different from the ones he'd already claimed or not. You really couldn't tell.

Mickey's teeth were chattering. "Where d-do we ride them?" he asked.

"All over," said Neil.

"How do we stay on?" Mickey said.

"We have reins," I said suddenly. I thought I'd just pretend with them for a minute.

"Yeah!" Neil said. "And when I whistle, they swim in and we get on." Neil whistled again.

Mickey was shaking with the cold. His coat sleeves hid his hands and he looked real little. "I w-wish w-we could," he said.

"Well, let's go," said Neil.

"Where?" said Mickey.

"Ride 'em," said Neil.

The three of us slid down the smooth side of the dune. Neil stood up and began loping along the water, bobbing up and down like he was riding a dolphin.

Mickey followed him. He pretended to hold reins and he made a high cawing sound. I didn't know what to do. This game seeemed so childish, but I really wanted to be with those guys. I didn't want to stay by myself and think about what had just happened at the shopping center. All of a sudden I took off running after Mickey and Neil.

I swear it felt like we really were riding dolphins that day, with the saltwater spraying us as we cantered down the beach. We rode through the cold misty air for the rest of the afternoon, until dark covered the dunes and the foghorn was blowing and the pilot ship was just a blinking light out at sea.

11

That night Neil ate dinner with us. Then he and Mickey and I played ghosts. One of us was a ghost who chased the other two around the house, causing them to panic and squeal. It was fun. I actually was a little scared, running and hiding.

On Sunday I rode with Mickey to a broken-down amusement park. We climbed around an abandoned Ferris wheel and sat on the grass and ate a fruit-and-nut mixture we'd bought at a health food store. We talked about when Pop was stationed in Germany and we always ate fresh-baked bread and took walks in the country

I stayed real close to Mickey all weekend. Playing with him helped keep my mind off that scene at the mall.

But by Sunday night I was starting to get a headache. I dreaded going to school the next day and seeing Jeanie and Paula and Stephanie.

"Mom, I think I'm sick," I said, stretched out in front of the TV.

Mickey was half stretched out beside me. He had a stomachache again. Mom was taking his temperature.

"What's wrong with you children?" Mom said. She sounded a little angry. I think she got angry when we got sick because it worried her. She felt my head.

"You're warm. When I'm through taking his temperature, I'll take yours."

Mickey was staring at a show about animal predators. A mountain lion was chasing a rabbit across the snow in slow motion to beautiful music. I watched it for a second and my spirits rose. But they fell again when I remembered those kids running from me. My face flushed. "I'm so hot," I said.

"Well, you probably have fever," Mom said with a big sigh. She reached over and took the thermometer out of Mickey's mouth.

"Good Lord, a hundred and one degrees. Cover up." Mom covered Mickey with the afghan. He stretched his neck to see the rabbit escape from the lion.

My temperature was ninety-nine degrees. "I've got two sick children," Mom said to Pop when he came in from the garage. He'd been changing the oil in his car.

"What's wrong with them?" he said.

"Fever, aches, and pains." She rocked in her rocker and shook her head. "Why did God ever give me children?" she said dramatically. Mickey shushed her so he could hear the narrator. I smiled at her. No school tomorrow. No popular kids. I was sick and happy.

The next morning I slept later than usual. I'd had a bad night; I'd dreamed that Jack and Jeanie were making fun of me on the school grounds.

I got out of bed and walked over and peeked in at Mickey. He was lying in bed, reading a Hardy Boys book.

"Are you still sick?" I said.

He nodded.

"Me too," I said. "I'm not going to school."

"Good. We can do stuff together."

"Okay." I hurried back to my room and got into bed.

In a few minutes Pop stuck his head in my doorway and said, "What's the report from sick bay?"

"I'm still sick," I said weakly.

"How about you, Bud?" Pop said, crossing the hall to Mickey's room.

"Me too," Mickey said.

Mom came upstairs and took our temperatures. Mickey's was the same. Mine was gone. "But my stomach hurts too," I said.

"Lord, stay in bed then," Mom said, and she went back downstairs.

I looked at my clock—eight o'clock. Time for those idiots to cross the intersection. I jumped up and ran to the bathroom. I raised the frosted glass window and looked toward the street. The wind blew cold through the open window. Then I saw them in their bright colors—a red down vest, a yellow ski jacket, blond hair blowing. I closed the window and ran shivering to Mickey's room.

"I'm freezing," I said as I crawled into his bed. I touched his flannel pajamas; they were white with little blue spacemen. He smelled warm.

"What do you want to do?" he said.

"I don't know."

"You want to play spies?"

"Sure."

"Wait here." He got up and walked to his dresser and got some paper and a pencil and brought them back to bed. The Banklys' dog began barking at a garbage truck.

"Write that down," I said.

I was lying on my side, still shivering from the outside cold. Mickey got situated beside me and wrote, "The dog barks." Mom started up the vacuum cleaner downstairs. "The machine!" he said.

"Write it down," I said. He wrote it down. And he wrote down other things we heard, like "The gulls caw" and "The plane flies."

Later we tried to decode our notes. We solved the case by figuring out that Laney Bankly was the secret boss of the other side. What other side—I don't know. None of it made any sense. But all morning we pretended that something very mysterious was taking place, and I didn't think at all about Jeanie or Stephanie or Paula or Jack or my breasts or my hair or my walk or my laugh.

12

On Tuesday Mickey still had fever. I didn't have any fever. But I was dying to stay home again. I still felt humiliated about Saturday.

"Can I stay home again too?" I asked Mom.

"You're not sick, honey."

"But I can stay with Mickey in case you want to go out."

"No, we have to take him to the doctor."

"No!" Mickey squealed from his room. He hated the doctor's.

"Yes, baby," Mom said.

"Ohhhh, damn!" Mickey said, hitting the bed with his fist.

"Baby, don't say damn!" Mom said. She sounded serious, but later while I was eating my cereal, I heard her laughing in the hall with Pop, telling him how Mickey had said "damn" and hit the bed.

I ate my cereal and wished I had a stomachache, too, so I could be with Mom and Pop today and not go to school and have to face those girls.

At eight o'clock I poked my head in Mickey's room. He was lying on his side, his eyes wide open, staring at the floor.

"Hi, squirt blossom. I'm not walking today. I'm riding my bike," I said.

He looked at me.

"Are you afraid of the doctor's?" I said.

He nodded.

"Pretend you're a spy and take notes."

He made a face like that was a dumb idea.

"Oh, do it. Think up a code and write your notes in it."

He shrugged.

"Come on, do it."

He made a face like "maybe."

"I'll race home when school's out," I said, and I blew him a kiss.

He said, "Yuk."

"'Bye, squirt blossom," I said, and left him.

When I got to school, I parked my bike and stood by the bike rack. I opened my science book and pretended to read.

As soon as the bell rang, I hurried into the building and sat at my desk. I glanced at Jeanie and Paula and Stephanie when they filed in.

"Hi, Hallie," Jeanie said.

"Hi, Hallie," Paula said.

They were acting like nothing had happened.

I nodded at them, then quickly turned my attention to finding some pages in my notebook.

I didn't talk or make jokes all morning. I dreaded lunchtime. I didn't know whether I should sit with Jeanie and them or not. I felt that if I didn't, I'd draw attention to myself, and that was the last thing I wanted to do. I wished I could just disappear and no one would remember I'd existed.

In the lunch line I watched Jeanie and Paula and Stephanie go over to our usual spot. I paid for my lunch and walked toward them. They were giggling as I sat down by Stephanie. While they ate they talked as usual about Jack and about Dennis, some guy Stephanie thought was cute. They didn't say anything about running from me on Saturday. Once Paula kind of laughed weird—she went "heh-heh-heh"—and Jeanie and Stephanie cracked up and looked at me, then acted like they were trying not to laugh. My face got hot, but I acted like things were normal. I hardly ate anything at all, but when I left the lunchroom, I felt sort of sick, like I'd eaten too much.

When the bell finally rang at three, I grabbed my books and charged out of class. When I pulled my bike out of the bike stand, Laney called to me. "Hallie, wait!"

"What?" I shouted. I waited impatiently for her to cross the blacktop.

"Do you want to do something this afternoon?" she panted.

"No, I can't," I said. "I have to take care of Mickey. He's sick. I'm in a hurry—I'll see you later." I got on my bike and sped out of the parking lot. I sure didn't want to hang out with Laney, not today or any day. That would make me feel like an even bigger reject than I already was.

When I got to our house, I dropped my bike on the grass and ran into the house. "Hi!" I called. "I'm home."

Mom stuck her head out from the kitchen. "Quiet, he's sleeping."

"What did the doctor say?"

"He doesn't know. We have to go back tomorrow."

Mom went back into the kitchen and I tiptoed up the stairs and peeked into Mickey's room. "Psss-t," I said. I looked toward the stairs to be sure Mom couldn't hear me.

"Psss-t," I said. He opened his eyes and smiled like he was really glad to see me.

Mickey stayed out of school all that week. I hated school. I had an upset stomach every morning before I left the house. I kept eating lunch with Jeanie and Paula and Stephanie because I didn't know how to stop. But I didn't act very funny anymore. I'd lost my confidence that day at the mall.

It was a relief to get home every day and be with Mickey. If Laney saw me in the yard and asked me to do something with her, I told her I had to take care of Mickey. He was waiting for me every afternoon, propped up in his bed.

The doctors still didn't know what was wrong with him. A few days before Thanksgiving, I heard Pop talking on the phone to my Aunt Mary in Daytona.

"Well, one of them thought it was a bladder infection," Pop was saying. "These damn civilian doctors can't figure anything out." I was standing in the upstairs hall, waiting to sneak into Mickey's room as a bandit and rob him and Bosco. I kneeled by the stair railing and listened to Pop's conversation.

"We may have to take him to Norfolk," he said. "It could be real serious. They want to run more tests on his kidneys. . . . Yeah, Lil's pretty distressed. Here, let me put her on."

My mother's voice was soft so I couldn't hear her. I took off my bandanna. I felt like I couldn't breathe. I was afraid. It wasn't the kind of fear I felt about going to school. This was different. This fear was deep and suffocating.

I opened the door to Mickey's room. He had the the covers pulled over his head, waiting for me to rob him.

"Hey, squirt, I'm not a bandit," I said.

The covers shook and he giggled. He still thought I was going to rob him.

"Mickey, come out."

There was the muffled sound of giggling again. Tears filled my eyes.

"Come out!" I shouted.

Mickey poked his curly head out from under the plaid blanket. His face was real red. Just seeing him made me so relieved.

"Put 'em up!" I shouted, raising fake guns. He squealed and covered his head again.

13

When I was clearing off the dinner table the next night, I asked Mom what was wrong with Mickey. She said she didn't know. I asked her what she guessed was wrong with him and she said, "I said I don't know. Now, run on and let me finish cleaning up."

I went in the living room and asked Pop how things were going with Mickey's tests. He said, "Fine."

When I played with Mickey that night, I stopped

whatever we were doing if he looked like he was exerting himself too much. At one point I asked him if he'd like me to read to him. "That's ridiculous," he said. "I know how to read."

Two days later Anne came home for the Thanksgiving holidays. I was happy—no school and plenty of Anne. Mickey was still sick, though. Thanksgiving Day he sat under a quilt on the couch and watched the Macy's parade on TV. Mom and Anne were talking softly in the kitchen. It was a cold day. The wind kept banging the screen door open and shut. Pop was bringing in wood for a fire. I was kneeling beside the fireplace lighting newspaper to get the kindling started.

"Well, how do they explain the last test?" I heard Anne say in the kitchen.

"They don't know. They're worried about—" Mom's voice got lower and I couldn't hear her. I stood up slowly and moved toward the kitchen. Mom saw me. She quietly closed the door to the living room.

I whirled around to Mickey. "What's wrong with you?" I said.

He looked up from the TV. "What?"

"What's your sickness?"

"I don't know." He said this in a grouchy way, like I shouldn't interrupt his program.

"What do the doctors say?" I said.

He shrugged and looked back at the TV. His attitude made me feel calmer. I sat on the couch next to him and watched the parade.

Pop came in and got the fire started. In a little while Mom and Anne came in from the kitchen and sat down.

"Hallie, are you still taking tap-dancing classes?" Anne said.

"No, she quit a few weeks ago," Mom said. "Isn't that a shame? She says the popular girls don't tap."

"Why don't you tap for us now?" Anne said.

"No," I said.

"Come on."

"No."

"Please."

"Oh, oooo-kay," I said, acting like I was doing them all a big favor. "Let me get my outfit." I ran up to my room and grabbed my black shiny shoes out of the closet and put them on. I grabbed my grass skirt and pulled it on over my jeans. My shoes made a lot of noise as I tapped down the stairs.

"Pop, put my record on, please," I said, poking my head around the corner. "It's in the yellow jacket."

Pop put on my record, and when the band music started, I tapped into the living room and over to the stone hearth. I tapped the hula, my grass skirt swaying from side to side. Everyone was smiling.

"Lord, she's on fire!" Mom suddenly yelled. An ember from the fire had landed on the back of my skirt and the grass was starting to smoke. I yanked down my skirt and Pop jumped up and stamped on it. I stamped on it too, though the fire was out. I kept stamping on it because it was a funny thing to do. Everyone was laughing.

"Hula Tapper Burns in Bizarre Mishap!" Anne said with tears running down her cheeks. Mom was laughing and saying, "Oh, Lord, dolly." Mickey got so worked up he started throwing his quilt around.

Slowly we came back to normal. Turkey and stuffing smells were coming from the kitchen. Red sunlight filled our living room. I got back on the couch close to Mickey and looked around at my family. I felt great. I loved making them all laugh so hard. None of us seemed to be worried about anything. Mom and Pop and Anne were smiling. Mickey looked bright and healthy. I was amazed that I had blown his illness so much out of proportion lately.

The Sunday after Thanksgiving Anne rolled my hair. I was hoping that rolling it would make it look silky like Jeanie's. I sat at the dresser, my head bowed, while Anne worked away.

"I hope this straightens it," I said. "So I won't look like a wild woman anymore."

Anne laughed and rubbed more gel into my hair.

"When your hair dries, just take the curlers out and comb it," she said. She picked up another hunk of hair and wrapped it around a pink foam-rubber curler. "You haven't said much about your friends," she said. "Are you good friends with the girl next door?"

"Not really. She's kind of weird."

"Weird how?"

"I don't know, but nobody likes her very much."

"Well, who are your friends?"

"There're some girls I used to be friends with, but, well, we have different personalities, sort of."

"What are they like?"

"They hang out mostly with seventh-grade boys, and just talk about clothes and making out and stuff like that."

"Sounds pretty boring."

"Yeah, it is," I lied.

"Some kids can be pretty shallow," Anne said as she pushed my head farther down to roll the very back.

"What's 'shallow' mean?"

"You know what it means. It means they don't have much imagination or they're not very deep."

"Do you think I'm shallow?" I said with my chin pressed against my chest.

"No, the opposite," she said. "Here, let me see." She put her hand under my chin and lifted my face.

"You're beautiful—you look like you're from *Star Wars*."

I looked in the mirror and squealed. "I'd better go show Mickey and Neil. I'll be back in a minute to help you pack."

I peeked into Mickey's room. He and Neil were playing a computer game. Neil was sitting on the floor next to the bed.

"Beep-beep," I said.

"Eek—a monster!" said Mickey.

"How are you doing, Neil?" I asked. I sat on the floor near him.

He smiled at me. "Fine."

"How are your turtles?"

"Great."

"That's amazing. Every turtle we ever had died of soft shell," I said.

"Tell her their names," Mickey said.

"Chlorophyll the First, Chlorophyll the Second, Chlorophyll the Third, Chlorophyll the Fourth, and Chlorophyll the Fifth," said Neil.

"Pretty good names," I said.

"What are you doing to your hair?" Neil said.

"Trying to straighten it out."

"I like it curly. It's like angel hair," he said.

"Oh, sure."

"Guess what," Mickey said. "Neil's moving to Rhode Island."

"When?"

"A week from tomorrow."

"Oh," I said. "Well, I'd better go help Anne pack."

I got up and walked back to our room, but it was empty.

"Anne, Anne!" I called down the stairs.

"They're loading the car," Mom yelled from the kitchen.

"I was supposed to help her pack," I whined. I plopped down on the top stair in the dark and held on to the banister, propping my head against the railing. I felt terrible. Anne was going back to Chapel Hill; Neil was moving to Rhode Island; and I had to go back to school tomorrow. I pulled myself up and went back to my room. I picked up one of Anne's bags and carried it downstairs.

14

Before I went to bed that night I took out my curlers. Sticky curls popped up all over my head. I pulled them to try and straighten them, but they popped back into place. There was no way my hair was ever going to be straight and silky like Jeanie's. I threw my comb down and yanked a green scarf out of a drawer and tied it around my head. I thought the scarf might flatten the curls out by morning.

I flopped down on my bed, feeling miserable. I wished Anne hadn't gone back to college so she could make my hair right.

I got up and tiptoed across the hall to Mickey's room. He was sleeping, but his lamp was still on. I walked to the end of his bed and touched a toe poking out from his covers. He didn't stir. He seemed so still and peaceful in the dim light. I wondered why the doctors couldn't figure out what he had.

I sat down at the foot of his bed. I wished I could stay with him and not have to go to school. I'd liked it in North Carolina one summer when we had a tree house and we ate at least two meals a day up in it. I'd liked it, too, when we played that we were riding dolphins with Neil. I wanted to do more things like that with him before it was too late and I *really* had to act mature. I eased myself onto Mickey's bed and crawled into the space between him and the wall. I worked my way under the covers and went to sleep beside him.

At dawn I felt Mickey shaking beside me.

"What's that on your head?" he sobbed. He didn't ask why I was sleeping in his bed.

I felt my scarf. "It's fixing my hair. Why are you crying?"

"My stomach hurts," he said. I should have gotten my mother then, but I didn't. I wanted to make him feel better myself.

"Here," I said, "just relax. You're all scrunched up. That's why it hurts." I tried to gently take his hands away from his stomach.

"Get Mom," Mickey said, breathing hard.

"I'll rub your head," I said. "That'll help you relax." I rubbed my hand across his forehead. He started crying harder. "Put your legs out straight and your hands down by your side."

He didn't do what I said.

"Mickey, do that. You need to relax your—"

"Get Mom," he breathed.

"Please, put your—"

Mickey's whole body jerked forward. I jumped up His head came forward and then it fell limply back onto the pillow. His eyes rolled back in his head. I screamed, "Mom!"

Mickey's hands were twitching. I screamed, "Mom! Mom!" His legs started jerking up and down.

Mom and Pop burst into the room. Mom grabbed Mickey and held him while Pop stumbled back to the hall and called an ambulance. Pop came back and sat with Mom. Mickey was still twitching a little. Mom held his arms, saying, "Okay, baby, okay, baby, okay, baby."

It seemed they had been that way for a long time when I heard a siren in the distance. It screamed louder and louder until it wound down in front of our house. Pop ran outside and came back with two ambulance men. They carried Mickey downstairs. Mom and Pop followed them. I pulled my parka on over my nightgown and slipped into my tennis shoes without tying them. I still wore my scarf as I hurried down the stairs after everybody. At the door, Pop turned to me and said, "Go on to school, baby. Everything will be all right."

I watched Mom get into the ambulance with Mickey while Pop got the car out of the garage. I stood in the cold and watched Pop follow the screaming ambulance down the street. I could hear the screaming long after the ambulance had turned the corner.

15

Mom and Pop didn't come home all day. And they didn't call me. I guess they thought I was in school, but I didn't go to school. I sat on the stairs and cried. I sat on Mickey's bed and cried. All morning I walked from room to room, crying. I felt like I was in some kind of shock. I couldn't figure out what had happened. I called the hospital in Holden Beach and asked if Mickey Pine had been checked in, but they couldn't give me any information. A few times I tried to get through to Anne, but she wasn't in her dorm.

Around noon I changed out of my nightgown. I ate some peanut butter off a spoon. Then I got a ball and bounced it on the back patio. It was gray and wet outside. I talked to myself while I bounced the ball. That helped a little bit. But when I stopped bouncing the ball and held it to my chest and listened to my hard breathing and the waves pounding the shore, I grew terrified. I ran inside the house like something was after me. I locked the doors and ran upstairs.

My room was quiet except for the sound of my clock. I grabbed a Dolly Parton record from Anne's record collection and put it on the stereo.

When the record was over, I heard noise downstairs and charged out of my room. Pop was in the downstairs hall. I ran down the stairs and before I said anything to him, I grabbed him and squeezed him till he nearly suffocated.

"Where is he? What's wrong with him?" I said. "Where is he, Pop?"

"Mom and Mickey are staying at the hospital in Norfolk for a little while," he said, rubbing my back. "Come on, let me get my coat off."

I stepped away from him. Pop took his coat off and hung it in the hall closet.

"What happened to him, Pop?"

"He had a seizure," Pop said.

"From what?"

Pop paused for a second. Then he said, "The doctors found a—a tumor in his lower abdomen."

"What's that? Cancer?" My voice went up.

"It's better just to call it a tumor," Pop said, putting his arms around me.

"Can they fix it?" I said.

"Well, first they have to find out what kind of tumor it is. Then they'll work on making him well."

"How do they find out?"

"He'll have an operation. They'll take out some of the tumor and study it. After that the doctors will know exactly what to do."

"Oh. When can I see him?" I said.

"Well, children under thirteen aren't supposed to visit. But I'll see if I can get you special clearance."

"How long will he be gone?" I started to sob. I pressed my face against Pop's sweater.

"Jesus," Pop said. "Don't cry. Let's go into the living room. Come on." He put his hand on my back and took me into the living room. Then he switched on a lamp and turned on the TV. The local news was on.

"At ease now, baby. Just sit down and calm down," Pop said. He motioned for me to sit on the couch. I sat beside him and we stared at the local news.

I don't know what the news was saying or why we were watching it. But we watched the local news until the CBS news came on. Then we watched the CBS news until Pop suggested we go out and get something to eat. Tears streaked my face. I'd been crying quietly during the news. Pop had known it, but he hadn't known what to do about it. For a while he had held my hand.

When we had our coats on, ready to go out the door to Kentucky Fried Chicken, Pop came up behind me and hugged me and said, "Don't worry, baby. I won't let anything happen to our boy."

We went out and picked up a box of chicken. We brought it back home and ate while we watched a TV movie. Finally I fell asleep in front of *Lou Grant,* exhausted from so much worrying.

16

Mom and Mickey had been gone for three days before Pop got permission for me to visit the hospital.

In class Thursday morning I was so nervous, I laughed at anything that was even a little bit funny.

"I'm leaving at twelve," I whispered to Jeanie when she passed me back a test paper. She shrugged like she didn't know why I was telling her that.

"My brother's in the hospital in Norfolk," I whispered.

Paula and Jeanie looked impressed. "What's wrong with him?" Jeanie said.

"He has a tumor."

Jeanie's eyes got wide. "Gross," she said.

"Girls," Mr. Edge said.

We were quiet for a minute.

"It's in his stomach," I whispered.

Paula and Jeanie made faces like "ugh."

"But they can fix it," I said quickly.

At five to twelve there was a knock on the door. Mr. Edge walked over to answer it. I smiled knowingly and closed my book.

"My father," I said.

"Hallie," Mr. Edge said, turning to me.

"I know. I'm coming." I pulled on my parka and grabbed my things.

"'Bye," I said, smiling at Jeanie and Paula and Stephanie.

"'Bye," they said.

I hurried out to the hall to join Pop.

The car seat was warm from the midday sun. I pulled down the sun visor and Pop turned on the radio.

"Oh, good, I see you brought Bosco," I said, looking over my shoulder.

"Yes."

"And the comics and Hardy Boys books?" I said, leaning over to peep into a bag on the backseat.

"Yes."

I hit my hand against the vinyl. "Darn, I wish we could have thought to bring Neil Larsen."

"Who?"

"Neil Larsen. Don't you remember—he was at our house on Sunday. He's Mickey's best friend." Pop nodded. "Well, he's moving next week," I said. "So Mickey might not get to see him again."

Pop didn't respond.

"You know Neil has five turtles and they're all named Chlorophyll?"

"I didn't know that," Pop said.

"Hey, maybe we should bring Mickey a turtle," I said. "We could get one on the way—at a Woolworth's, easy. What do you think?"

"He's very sick, Hallie."

"I know."

"He can't play with a turtle."

"I didn't mean play with one," I said. "I meant watch it."

Pop didn't say anything.

"I didn't mean play with one," I said, and I turned and looked out the side window.

We parked in the parking lot of Robert E. Lee Memorial Hospital and walked to the entrance marked PEDIATRICS. Some ladies and little children were sitting in the waiting room. We passed a reception desk and a gift shop. I followed Pop down the hall to the elevator. He was carrying Bosco and the bag of books. I was zipping and unzipping my parka.

We got into the elevator. Pop pushed 4. When we got off the elevator, my heart started pounding hard. I didn't like the smell in the hall. We passed a little girl in a wheelchair. It made me nervous. I grabbed Pop's elbow and held on to him as he led me down the hall.

We stopped outside a closed door.

"Is this it?" I said.

Pop put his hands on my shoulders. "Now, talk softly and don't touch anything. He'll have a tube going into his arm, but don't let that upset you. It doesn't hurt him."

"What do you mean—" I said. But Pop was already opening the door.

The venetian blinds were slanted down and sunlight streamed onto the floor. My mother was sitting in a chair reading *Family Circle*. She looked alarmed when we walked in.

"Shhhhh," she said, rising.

I glanced at Mickey. He was sleeping. I went quickly over to my mother. Pop kissed her. "Why's he—" I said.

"Talk softly," Pop said.

"Why's he sleeping?" I whispered.

"He's tired," Mom said.

"Oh." I walked over and leaned against the windowsill. I looked around the room. I kept fiddling with the zipper on my parka.

"How is he today?" Pop said.

"He's real exhausted."

"When will he wake up?" I whispered. Mom walked over to Mickey and lightly stroked his forehead. She said in a sweet voice, "Baby, dolly's here."

I giggled. Pop looked at me.

Mickey's eyes opened. "Come say hi." Mom held out her hand to me.

I was smiling as I walked to him. "Hi," I said. Mom moved away.

He smiled. I leaned toward him. His face was white and tired-looking. I saw the tube going into his arm, and I felt like I was going to be sick.

"Hi," I said.

"Hi."

"We brought Bosco and some Hardy Boys and some comics." I grabbed a couple of comics out of the bag and handed them to Mickey. I picked Bosco up from the floor where Pop had put him. I held the bear up and waved his paw. "Hi, squirt," I said in Bosco's voice.

Mickey laughed a little laugh. Tears came to my eyes, but I wiped them fiercely with my wrist. "Get well soon, so we can play," I said like Bosco.

"Remember—" Mickey said softly.

"What?" I dropped Bosco by the bed and leaned in closer.

Mickey didn't answer for a few seconds.

"What?" I said.

Pop put his hand on my shoulder and tried to pull me back. "The boy's pretty tired—" he said.

"Wait!" I tried to shake Pop's hand off my shoulder. "What?" I whispered to Mickey.

"When we rode dolphins with Neil."

"Yes."

"We can do that."

"Say good-bye now," Pop said.

Mickey put one of the comic books in front of his face like he was going to read it. The comic book shook and I knew he was crying.

"Say good-bye—" Pop said, pulling me back.

"No," I said, and I tried to hold on to Mickey's covers. Pop put his arms around me and pulled me back. "No!" I screamed, and I flailed my arms, trying to grab for Mickey's bed. My mother rushed to protect Mickey. Pop dragged me, crying, out into the hall. I was fighting him, trying to get back into Mickey's room. A couple of nurses charged down the hall toward us. "She's not supposed to be in here!" one yelled, pointing at me.

I was sobbing and fighting with Pop.

"Sir, she's not supposed to be in here!"

Pop put one arm around me and gripped my left

shoulder with his hand and steered me forward. "Move out of my damn way!" he said to the nurses.

Pop guided me out of the building and out to the parking lot. When I got in the car, I slouched against the door with my hands in my pockets. I stopped crying.

Pop didn't say one word until we turned onto the highway. Then he said, "I'm sorry. I shouldn't have taken you."

"Yes, you should have," I said, my voice cracking. He didn't say anything else for the rest of the ride. I didn't either.

When we pulled up to our house, Pop told me to go play until dinnertime. He talked to me like I was about five years old. I got out of the car and saw Laney coming off her porch. Dammit, I thought, I didn't want to deal with her now.

Laney and Pop said hi to each other, then Pop went into the house. Laney stood there looking at me, like she was waiting for me to say something. I leaned against the car, clenching my fists in my pockets.

"Did you visit Mickey?" she said.

I nodded

"Well?"

I didn't say anything.

"How was it?" she said.

I shrugged.

"Is he better?"

I shrugged again.

"Well, if there's anything I can do . . ." she said.

"No," I said.

She stood there like she was still waiting for me to say something about him.

"I don't want to talk about him," I said coldly.

Laney nodded, then she said good-bye and turned and left me. My anger at her sort of caved in as I watched her lumber across the yard.

I pushed myself away from the car and walked slowly to the house.

When I got inside I found Pop sitting on the couch, staring at nothing. I stood near him and said, "Pop, I'm sorry."

"Don't be sorry," he said. "It's my fault."

"No, it's mine," I said. "I won't act that way again."

He didn't say anything.

"When you take me again, I won't act that way," I said.

"Okay, baby. Let's not talk about it anymore. Click on the TV."

I stood there for a second, not sure what to do. I wanted to talk about it. But I started thinking maybe he was right—what was there to talk about? Maybe we should just watch TV. I turned on the TV and went over and sat next to him as close as I could without crowding him. We watched an *Ironside* rerun. And we didn't talk about Mickey or my behavior in the hospital for the rest of that evening.

17
_____

The next morning, first thing when I got up, I walked to Pop's room and asked him when I could go see Mickey again.

"Maybe in a while," he said.

"When?" I said.

"I don't know." He didn't look at me. He was buttoning his shirt and tying his tie. I stood in the doorway to his room.

"Tomorrow?" I said.

"No," he said. He got his change off the dresser and dropped it in his pocket.

"The next day?" I said.

"No," said Pop. He put on his watch. Then he walked by me and patted my head and said, "Let's get some breakfast." And he left the room.

I didn't want any breakfast. I didn't have an appetite.

"In a few days?" I called to Pop from the top of the stairs. But he didn't hear me. Or he was pretending not to.

That morning in class I stared out the window thinking about Mickey crying behind his comic book. It killed me to think he was sad. I wanted to be with him, help take care of him. I remembered when he was in kindergarten and I was in third grade. Every day on the school bus I'd save him a seat. When he got on the bus I'd see him standing at the front, stretching his neck, looking for me. I felt like he was looking for me now from his hospital bed. Suddenly I wanted to crash through the window of the classroom—make splinters and chunks of glass fly everywhere. Bleeding, I'd take off running to Norfolk. Nothing would stop me.

At lunchtime I stood in line, feeling terrible. I hated being at school. I was having to go through the motions of being there, but my heart and my mind were feeling wild, remembering Mickey and the comic book. I felt like throwing my head back and howling. But instead I had to stand in line and put a bowl of Jell-O and a plate of macaroni on my tray. I had to pay fifty cents and walk like a normal person across the room to a table. By force of habit, I started to pull out a chair next to Stephanie. Jeanie was giggling about something—I don't know what—but suddenly her stupid giggle made me sick. I felt like I couldn't bear sitting with her and Stephanie and Paula and listening to them talk.

I let go of the chair and walked to the other end of the table and sat by myself. I felt like I was in a sad, serious world far away from their gossip, their boyfriends, and their jokes. I started to take a bite of Jell-O, but I stopped. I felt like I was going to vomit. I got up and walked over to Mr. Edge and very calmly said, "I have to go to the girls' room." He looked at me and nodded.

As I walked across the lunchroom I saw Laney sitting at a table alone. She looked up at me. I quickly looked in another direction.

I got to the bathroom just in time to be sick. Then I ran some cold water and splashed it over my face as I cried.

The bathroom door opened. I jumped, reaching for a paper towel. I pressed the rough sand-colored paper against my eyes.

"Hi," someone said.

I looked around. It was Laney. I nodded at her, sniffing.

"Are you okay?" she said. I nodded, but tears started coming down my face again. She moved forward a little and stood near me. "Are you upset about Mickey?" she said.

I nodded again. I felt like I couldn't talk.

"You shouldn't worry if you feel like crying," she said.

"But I can't—can't cry in school," I gasped.

"Cry a lot in here before you go back to class," she said.

"But I feel like crying in class and at lunch, all the time," I said, pressing the paper towel to my eyes.

"Maybe you should leave school," she said in a small voice. I looked at her. Her eyes were wet.

"But you're not allowed to just leave," I said.

"When my father first moved away, I left school a few times," she said. I was surprised to hear this from Laney. I'd never pictured her as the kind of person who would skip school.

"Did they catch you?"

She nodded.

"What happened?"

"I had to see a counselor," she said.

"Oh. I wish—wish I could leave," I said, gasping for breath.

"Why don't you? It'll make you feel better," she said.

"Okay, I—I think I'll go home."

Laney opened the door to the girls' room and looked out in the hall. "You could go now," she said.

"Okay," I said, and I slipped past her out the door. I started walking fast. I hurried past the lunchroom, past my classroom, and out of the building.

It was beautiful outside. I ran to my bike, jumped on, and took off. Riding home, I was surprised that I'd told Laney what I was feeling, and I was surprised that doing that had made me feel better. I stood up on my pedals, feeling free in the cool blue air.

When I got to our house, I dropped my bike on the grass and charged inside. I called "Mom!" There was no answer. I called "Pop!" but he wasn't there either. I grabbed the phone and dialed Anne's dormitory. But the phone rang until a girl finally answered and said Anne was in class.

When I hung up, the house felt lonely and scary. I ran outside again. I stood on the lawn, wondering what to do, afraid the neighbors might see me. I decided to go to the beach, and I took off running.

I ran over the cold white sand toward the dunes. I grabbed a stick from the sand and started climbing a dune like I was a mountain climber, conquering a mountain. Except I started crying again as I climbed. I couldn't get away from my feelings. I collapsed when I got to the top of the dune and curled up on my side, crying like a baby. The wind blew hard, but the sun warmed me. I wiped my face and closed my eyes. I listened to the waves hitting the shore and to the wind. I fell asleep.

I dreamed we were living back in North Carolina and Tommy Barron's red setter could talk and we were jumping in some leaves—me and Mickey and Tommy's dog. I half opened my eyes. The sand felt cold and damp. I felt like Mickey was close by— Mickey and Tommy's dog. I looked up. Someone was walking down the beach. Mickey.

I scrambled down the side of the dune. I took off, desperately running toward him. Then I stopped. It wasn't Mickey. It was Pop.

When Pop got to me, he grabbed my arms and yanked me to him. "What the hell are you doing!" he said. He was real red in the face. I couldn't answer.

"The school called my office and they called the hospital. What are you doing?" he shouted.

"Playing," I said. My teeth started to chatter. "Pl-playing."

"Come on," he said. He straightened up and put his hand on my back and gave me a shove. Our shoes squeaked in the sand as we walked home without talking.

18

When we got to our house, Pop and I stamped our feet on the porch. The house was cold and dark inside. Pop turned on a lamp.

"How's Mickey?" I said. Pop went into the kitchen and opened a cabinet door to look for food.

"How is he?" I said.

"He had his surgery this morning."

"He did? Did they take out the tumor?"

"Some of it, baby. Now he'll have to have some treatments to shrink the rest of it and keep it from spreading."

"What's that mean?"

"He's okay. He just needs to get his strength back. Then they'll start the treatments."

"How long will that be?"

"I don't know. You want tuna?"

"No. When do you think he's coming home?"

"If I knew, I'd tell you." Pop stood looking at the shelf for a long time. I think he didn't want to look at me.

"What do the doctors say?"

"They don't know," Pop said.

"Well, why doesn't anybody know anything!" I shouted.

"Shhh," Pop said, turning to look at me. "Calm down. We have to be patient—" He turned to look at the shelf again.

"Not me," I said. But Pop ignored me; he was moving cans around.

"Vienna sausages?" he said.

"*Nooo,*" I said. I wandered into the living room and flounced down on the sofa.

"I don't have to be patient," I murmured. I picked my ball up from the sofa and heaved it across the room. The ball hit a small table in the corner, knocking it over. I jumped up.

"What the hell!" Pop said. He stood in the doorway and looked at me angrily.

"I'm sorry," I said, setting the table back up.

"Go up and take a bath," he said. "Then we'll eat."

After I took my bath, Pop and I sat in front of the news and ate hot dogs and soup from TV trays. When Pop was finished, he said, "I have to go upstairs and make some phone calls; I'll be right back."

"Okay," I said.

I was watching *The Odd Couple* when Pop came back downstairs. He turned down the TV, sat at the end of the sofa, and took one of my bare feet in his hands. He shook my foot and looked at me.

"How would you like to go visit Aunt Mary and Uncle Bert in Daytona Beach for a while?" he said.

I took my foot back from him. "Why?" I said.

"Well, Mom and I are going to be in Norfolk a lot, and Anne can't leave school right now."

"Go by myself?"

"Yes."

"For how long?" I said.

Pop didn't answer. He was staring at *The Odd Couple* with the sound turned down. I stood up.

"For how long?" I said. Pop shook his head.

"You want me to spend Christmas there?"

He nodded.

"But I want to spend Christmas with the family," I said.

"I think it would be better if you went to your aunt's."

"No!" I screamed. "I want to be with Mickey and

the family. We can all visit him. Pop, we can!"

"I think it would be better if you went to Mary's," Pop said quietly. He put his head in his hands.

"Why?" I screamed. I dropped on my knees in front of him and grabbed him around the neck. "What's happening to him?" I yelled. Pop pulled my hands away.

"Pop!" I screamed, clutching for him.

"Don't," he said, pushing me back. "Don't, d—" His mouth twisted and tears came out of his eyes. I let go of him. His hands covered his face and he sobbed. I'd never seen Pop cry before. I touched his hair. He reached up and patted my hand without looking. Then he got up off the sofa and went into the kitchen. I followed him and watched him from the doorway. He blew his nose, then turned on the fire underneath the kettle.

"Pop?" I said.

"Why don't you go on up to bed?" he said in a soft voice.

"Is he going to die?" I said.

Pop shook his head. "They have treatments. He'll get better."

"Are you sure?"

Pop nodded. "Go on up," he said.

"Okay, good night," I said. I climbed the stairs, holding tight to the banister.

In the dark I climbed onto my bed and curled up

under my covers. I wasn't sure Pop was telling the truth when he said Mickey would get better. I felt like our house was flying apart. I buried my head under my pillow and cried. I have to see Mickey, I thought, I have to see him, I have to.

19

The next morning I crept out of bed early. I heard Pop moving around downstairs. I tiptoed to the hall phone and dialed Anne's number. A girl answered and I asked for Anne Pine. In a minute, Anne's sleepy voice said, "Hello?"

"Hi, it's Hallie," I whispered.

"What's wrong?"

"I—I—" I started to cry. I tried to get control of myself. I breathed heavily for a few seconds, then I tried again. "Did you know Mickey had an operation?"

"Yes," she said. "I talked to Mom yesterday."

"What did she say? Did she say he would be okay?"

"Well, she said there's a good chance he'll get better."

"How will he get better?" I said.

"They can give him treatments, like chemo-therapy."

"What's that?"

"That means giving him some strong drugs."

"Do you believe he'll get better?"

"Yes!" she said. She sounded a little cross.

"Did you know I have to go to Daytona Beach?" I said.

"Who said?"

"Pop told me last night. Why do I have to leave?" I said, my voice cracking.

"It's probably so Mom and Dad can be with Mickey together."

"Why can't I be with him too?"

"I heard you got real upset when you visited him," she said.

"But I won't next time," I said.

"Well, you might, and that wouldn't be good for you or him. Or anybody."

"So you think I should go away too? I didn't think *you* would think that," I said.

"Well, it just might be easier for you—until he gets well."

"No, it wouldn't," I said. "Mom and Pop think

I'm a baby. But I'm not. I want to stay and help take care of him."

She sighed. "Well, talk to Dad, not me," she said. "Tell him you want to stay."

"I did."

"Try again, and try to act more grown-up when you ask him."

"I do act grown-up," I said, my feelings hurt.

"Okay. I know you do. Call me tomorrow," she said.

"When are you coming home?"

"I'm not sure."

"'Bye," I said.

"'Bye. Be good, now," she said. "Help Mom and Dad."

I hung up. Then I went in the bathroom and washed my face. I wanted to act mature and normal so Pop would listen to me when I told him I didn't want to go away. I went back to my room and brushed my hair at Anne's dresser. I looked pale and wasted from so much crying. I picked up a bottle of Anne's Cover Girl and rubbed some on my face. I scrounged through her drawer till I found some old blush, and I powdered it on my cheeks. There wasn't much I could do for my swollen eyes.

I dressed and went downstairs. I walked into the kitchen. Pop was sitting at the table, doing nothing in particular.

"Hi," I said.

He nodded and squinted at me.

I took some juice out of the refrigerator and poured it. "Would you like some?" I asked.

He shook his head. I carried my glass over to the table and sat next to him.

"Going to Norfolk soon?" I said casually.

"Yes," he said.

I nodded and sipped my juice.

"We have to make your reservations," he said.

"Oh, I wanted to talk with you about that," I said, trying to stay calm. "I think it would be better if I stayed here with you guys and helped out."

He shook his head.

"I think—" I said, my voice starting to rise, "that I'd be more help—"

"Baby, you have to go to your aunt's."

"But I don't want to!"

"You'll have a good time there."

"No, I won't." My lip started trembling.

"Let's not argue about it," Pop said.

"But, Pop, I want to stay and visit Mickey," I said.

"No, baby, we think—"

"Please!" I yelled, standing up. I couldn't control myself now. "Let me!"

He shook his head.

"Yes!" I shrieked, pounding my fist on the table. "Yes!"

Pop covered his ears, then he dropped his hands

and looked at me, "Please, help me by doing what I ask—"

"But—" I didn't know what to say. He was looking at me like he might cry again. I stood there staring at him with tears running down my face. He got up and walked over to the phone. He asked information for the number of Eastern Airlines.

I couldn't believe it. Just a little while ago, talking to Anne, it had seemed like all I had to do was tell Pop maturely that I didn't want to go to my aunt's. Now I was crying like a six-year-old, and he was making plane reservations.

"Flight three fifty-six?" he said. "She'll pick up the ticket Monday when we check in. Thanks." This was a nightmare. I couldn't control anything that was happening.

Pop hung up. "I'm going to the hospital now. Go on to school," he said.

"I don't have school. It's Saturday."

"Oh." He looked at me like he didn't know what to do.

"I guess I'll have to go with you to Norfolk," I said evenly.

"No, no, you stay with—" He didn't finish. He glanced at our phone list and dialed.

"What are you doing? Who are you calling?" I said.

"Hello, Ruth? Bob Pine," he said. "Can Hallie stay around your house today?"

He was talking to Laney's mother. "Okay, I'll send her over in a few minutes." He hung up.

"Pop!" I cried.

"Get dressed," he said absently.

"I *am* dressed," I said, surprised that he didn't see that. He didn't say anything else. He got up and walked out of the kitchen. I threw myself down in a chair. It's no use, I thought—he doesn't see me or hear me anymore.

20

A half hour later I was standing on Laney's doorstep. The front door opened. "Oh, darling," Mrs. Bankly said. "Go on up. Laney's in her room."

I climbed the stairs to Laney's room and found her sitting on her bed, surrounded by a bunch of magazines—*Seventeen, Glamour, People*. She looked up at me and smiled.

"I'm making a collage," she said.

"What's that?"

"It's a collection of different pictures pasted together. You want to help?"

I nodded and sat on the floor next to her bed. She was cutting a model out of *Glamour*.

"I like Brooke Shields in this blazer," she said. "I'm putting clothes I like and models I like and celebrities I like in the collage. And then I'm adding the names of movies and stuff like that. You can cut stuff out from this one if you want to."

She handed me a *Seventeen*. It was the same issue I'd read with Anne the day we'd moved last August. Leaning against her bed, I thumbed through it till I came to the picture of the girl in the red terry-cloth top. I remembered looking at this picture while Mickey was bothering me, acting like a dog.

I held the picture up to Laney. I said, "I like—I like—" I tried to say "this," but the damn waterworks came on. I pressed my face against her bedspread.

She didn't say anything for a second. Then she said, "I like that. Here, I'll cut it out." She took the magazine from me. "You can look at this one." I raised my face from the spread and took a *Glamour* from her. Without saying anything, she moved a box of Kleenex over to my side of the bed.

Laney cut out her pictures and I glanced around her room. On her bedside table were two really hard books—*Franny and Zooey* and *Catch-22*. They had bookmarks in them like Laney was in the middle of reading them. I didn't think anyone knew she was that smart. She didn't get very good grades. I thought maybe someday I'd tell Laney's teacher the truth about Laney.

Laney closed her magazine. "You want to ride around?" she said. I shrugged.

"We could go to the football field," she said. "I know Jack and Jeanie sometimes play football there on Saturday with their friends."

Laney studied the lives of Jeanie and that crowd like they were movie stars. She should put them in her collage, I thought.

"Wanna go?" she said.

"No, I don't really want to."

"Oh, come on," she said, smiling. "We can just ride over there and check it out, then come home."

I could tell she really wanted to go. "Okay," I said. I pulled myself up. She jumped up and debated a second about her outfit. She changed from her blue sweater to her burgundy sweater, then she led the way downstairs and outside.

We got our bikes and I drove behind Laney to the ballfield. I felt like I was wasting time. I had only two days left before I had to go to my aunt's in Florida. I didn't want to go down there alone. My aunt and uncle lived in the middle of a retirement neighborhood. When Mickey and I visited them together, we found things to do like go to the Dairy Queen or play putt-putt golf. But I couldn't do that stuff without him. I'd go crazy, missing him, worrying about him.

Laney turned in to the school. I followed her. We stopped and parked our bikes. The bleachers were empty except for Jeanie's gang. A few of them looked in our direction as we crossed the field.

"Where do you want to sit?" Laney said when we got to the bleachers.

"I don't care," I said.

"How about there?" she said, pointing.

"Okay." I followed her up an aisle and we sat on a gray wooden bench. We weren't far from Jeanie and Jack and the others. The guys seemed to be taking a break from playing football. Everyone was ignoring us. I figured the girls must have written me off for good yesterday when I didn't eat lunch with them. But I really didn't care. I was too concerned about Mickey.

Laney looked at them over her shoulder. Then she turned back to me, excited. "Who's that cute guy sitting with Paula?"

"I don't know," I said. She looked back at them. "Hey, I'm cold," I said, trying to get her attention. "Maybe we should go. There's nothing to watch. They're not playing."

The voices above us were getting louder. They were all laughing about something. "Hey!" a boy yelled. I stiffened. I knew that yell was directed at us. I didn't want to look, but Laney turned around. "What?" she said.

"You girls want a cigarette?" It was a seventh grader, one of the guys who'd been at the mall that day. Everyone was looking down at us as he held out a pack of Winstons. I figured the other girls must have refused his offer, so now he was making a joke by asking us.

"No, thanks," I said.

"Sure!" Laney said at the same time.

"All right!" he said. The other guys whooped. The girls booed. Laney jumped up. I stood up slowly and followed her up the bleachers to where they all sat. Laney reached for the cigarette. That idiot, I thought, she doesn't know how to smoke. Laney held the cigarette in her mouth while the guy lit it. Then she inhaled deeply and blew out the smoke. I guess she does know how to smoke, I thought. I wished she would turn away then and leave them. And she started to, but one of the guys said, "Can you smoke two at the same time?"

"Hey, right!" Jack said.

"Give her another one!" Jeanie said, laughing. They were making fun of her. Laney hesitated.

"Come on," I said softly to her. "Let's go." I pulled a little on her arm, and she dropped the cigarette she was holding. We walked down the bleachers together.

At first the guys said, "Hey, you girls!" and Jeanie and the other girls booed. But they were all laughing as we walked away. It wasn't any big thing to them. By the time we got to the bottom of the bleachers, I could hear them talking about getting their ball game back on. I figured by the time we got to our bikes, they would have completely forgotten us.

"Let's go back to your house," I said at the bike rack. As we rode home I was thinking that Jeanie and her friends were really babies, shallow babies. I knew little kids who were more mature than them; Mickey and Neil Larsen, for instance. And Laney wasn't immature and shallow like those kids either. She was just lonely.

When we parked in Laney's yard, I said, "I think those kids are dumb."

Laney nodded faintly. I knew she wasn't really convinced yet.

As we climbed the stairs to Laney's porch, I looked toward the beach. The sky was cold and gray and the fog was starting to come in—the same kind of day as the day I'd been embarrassed at the mall and I'd come home and played with Mickey and Neil. But now Mickey wasn't down by the dunes. He was far away in a hospital bed and suddenly it made me crazy thinking of that tube going in his arm. I leaned against the porch railing, feeling wild.

"Are you okay?" Laney said. She was holding the door open.

I shook my head no, and walked on into her house

21

After lunch, Laney and I watched gymnastics on TV. She thumbed through her magazines to cut out more pictures. Every time I heard a car drive down the street, I jumped up and looked out the window. At around four o'clock, I spied our car.

"I have to go," I said. I grabbed my parka from a chair and said, "Thanks. I'll see you tomorrow."

"Good," Laney said, smiling at me.

I charged out the front door and ran to our driveway. My heart leaped—it was Mom! She got out of the car and I danced up to her.

"Hi!" I said, putting my arms around her shoulders. But she really didn't hug me back. I let go of her. "Why are you here?" I said. "Can you stay?"

She reached in the car for her bag. "Just tonight," she said. "Dad's going to stay at the hospital tonight."

"Oh, good, I'm glad to see you."

She patted my back and we walked toward the house. I skipped along beside her.

I followed Mom into the house. She dropped her suitcase in the living room and crossed her arms.

"It's chilly in here!" she said. She walked to the hall and adjusted the thermostat, then she walked to the kitchen. I was right behind her.

"Pop said Mickey had his operation," I said.

She looked around the kitchen like she wasn't sure where she was. She opened the refrigerator door.

"How is he, Mom?" I said.

She turned around and looked at me, holding the fridge door open. Her eyes were opened wide. "Fine!" she said. Then she looked back in the refrigerator and said, "Lord, there's nothing in here."

"Can I go see him?" I said.

Mom closed the refrigerator door. "Not now, honey," she said.

"*Why not?*"

"You're not old enough," she said.

"I'm old enough!" I said, following her into the living room.

She picked her coat up off the sofa. "Let's go!" she said, walking toward the door.

"Where?" I said, suddenly excited. To the hospital?

She turned back to me and talked like we were in a conspiracy. "The mall. We'll eat dinner at the cafeteria!" I looked at the clock over the mantelpiece. It was only four-fifteen. We never ate dinner this early.

"Mom—"

"Come on," she said and she opened the door. I followed her to the car.

As we drove to the mall, Mom played the car radio and hummed along with it. I tried to talk with her again.

"Mom, do I have to go to Aunt Mary's?"

She nodded and started singing the radio song, instead of humming it.

"Why?" I said, raising my voice. "I want to stay here and visit Mickey. I'm old enough!"

"Children under thirteen aren't supposed to visit the patients," she said.

"But I visited before."

"We broke the rule. We can't do that again."

"Can't Pop get me special clearance again?"

She shook her head and started singing again.

"Oh, why not!" I whined and I slapped the car seat. But she ignored me.

We parked and walked into the K & W cafeteria and stood in line. Mom strained to see what dishes were posted.

"What do you want?" she said

"I don't care."

"The fish cakes here are delicious," she said

I pushed my tray down the row and pointed to turkey and stuffing.

Mom paid and we walked over to a table. We took our dishes off our trays and sat down amid the sounds of clattering dishes and people talking. I took a bite of cranberry sauce. "Mom, have Mickey's treatments started?" I said.

She shook her head and cut her fish cakes. Her hands were trembling. "Isn't this fun?" she said. "Afterward we'll do some shopping. I'll buy you everything you want!" I didn't want her to buy me everything I wanted. This was crazy. She'd never acted this way before. I put my fork down slowly and stared at her. I watched her hands shake as she took a bite of her fish cake and suddenly I absolutely knew the truth. *Mickey was dying.*

"Do you have a bathing suit?" she said. A busboy came by and picked up our trays. I stared at Mom.

"We'll get you one for Daytona!" she said, not waiting for my answer. "Eat your turkey. Don't you like turkey?"

I couldn't answer her I couldn't talk. I couldn't

pick up my fork. But she didn't seem to notice as she pushed her chair back and stood up. She pulled on her coat and took a last sip of iced tea before she walked away from the table.

I stumbled up after her and we quickly weaved in and out between the tables, crossing the loud room. We went out the exit and onto the Muzak-filled concourse. "Silver Bells" was playing over the loudspeaker. I was in a daze as I walked after her. *Mickey was going to die.*

"Let's go in here!" Mom said, leading me into the Young Smart Shop, the most expensive girls' store at the mall. We'd never shopped before in places like this.

"Can I help you?" a teen-age girl said.

"If you would," my mother said, "that would be so kind. She needs a bathing suit."

"Going south for the winter?" the girl said.

"Oh, yes!" said my mother.

The music in the store was playing "The Little Drummer Boy." I turned away from the salesgirl and Mom. My face was so tense from trying not to cry that I could hardly breathe.

The girl asked my size. I managed to say "Twelve," and she led us to the twelves. Mom yanked a blue dotted-swiss bikini and a denim two-piece off the rack. "Here you go!" she said, handing them to me. I don't think she knew what she was handing me. I clutched the suits. In the dressing room, I fought to keep from sobbing as I peeled off my clothes. Shivering, I stepped into the bikini. It didn't fit because I had no breasts.

I got back into my clothes and grabbed the denim suit without trying it on and carried it back to Mom.

"This one?" she said.

I nodded. The bathing suit cost thirty dollars. I didn't even know if it fit. But Mom paid for it, then she said, "Let's go!" real merrily, and I followed her out onto the concourse.

"You want some ice cream?" she said. *Ice cream.* I didn't want her to keep acting this way. I didn't want ice cream. *Mickey was dying.* Looking at her, I shook my head. Tears came into my eyes and my chin started to quiver.

"Stop that now," she said. "Come on." She walked ahead of me.

I followed her through Thalhimer's and Ivy's and Sears and Penney's. I hated being at the mall, going up and down the escalators. Mom didn't stop to look at anything, except in Thalhimer's she stopped at the cosmetic counter and sprayed sample perfumes on her wrists and rubbed sample lotions on her hands. She told me to smell them all. It was like a crazy dream—smelling perfumes, walking through the crowded stores, Christmas music playing, the Salvation Army Santa Claus, kids skating on ice in the center of the mall; and all the time both of us knowing Mickey was dying, knowing it for sure, but not rushing to be with him, not saying anything about it, not comforting each other, not ripping the displays apart and screaming our bloody heads off.

22

It was after eight when Mom and I got home. She went to use the phone in the kitchen and I climbed the stairs to my room. I closed my door and turned on my lamp and sat on my bed. I looked at my hands. A giant darkness seemed to hover above me and below me. Only where I was sitting, looking at my hands in the lamplight, was there color and movement and life.

"Mickey's dying," I said in a quiet voice. I felt very calm when I said it. "My brother's dead," I said. "Did you know he died?" I said. "He's going to die,"

I said. Any way I said it, it sounded as silvery and sharp as a blade. I pictured myself telling Neil Larsen, "Mickey died." Calling up Tommy Barron, that friend of Mickey's in North Carolina, and saying, "Mickey Pine died in December."

I heard my mother come upstairs. I got up and opened my door and walked softly down the hall. I looked in her room. She was sitting at her dresser, putting cold cream on her face. I wished I could go to her and hug her, squeeze her to bits. I wanted to say, Mom, can I see Mickey before he dies? I stepped into her room. "Hi," I said in a small tight voice.

She looked at me in her mirror. "What?" she said. She started wiping the cold cream off her face with a tissue.

"Can I go see Mickey before—" I couldn't say "he dies" to Mom. I just couldn't say it right then. It was different from saying "die" alone in my room.

"What?" she said.

"Can I go see Mickey before I go to Daytona Beach?"

She shook her head sadly. She wasn't pretending to be happy anymore. Her face was oily from her cream and she looked tired.

"Do you think if I went to the hospital, but"—I raised my hand to stop her objection—"but I didn't go *in* his room—I only stood in the hall and looked in, would anyone mind?"

"You can't stand in the hall," she said.

"Could I call him?"

"No, I don't think so."

"Why not?" I was angry. This was a good idea—to call him. She just wasn't being fair!

"First, there's no phone in his room. And second, if you talked to him, you'd get upset and then you'd upset him. You'd cry when you had to hang up." She was talking softly, enunciating her words clearly. *Why* hadn't I acted more normal the other day at the hospital, instead of going berserk, I thought. I'd ruined everything by screaming and crying. They'd *never* trust me again.

"You won't give me another chance?" I said.

She sighed and screwed the top to her cold-cream jar back on, not looking at me now.

"Mom—"

Her head was down. "Please," she said.

I turned and went back to my room.

The next morning the phone woke me up. I heard Mom talking in the hall. I jumped out of bed and opened my door. She put the receiver back on the hook.

"Who was that?" I said.

She looked at me without saying anything for a second.

"Who was that, Mom?"

"Oh, it was just Dad. It wasn't important." She

turned and walked quickly back to her room. I followed and watched her take a dress from her closet.

"Are you going now?" I said.

With her back to me, she said, "Yes, I think so."

"Me too," I said. I ran back to my room, yanked off my nightgown, and pulled on my jeans and a T-shirt. I started to leave, but ran back to my drawer and pulled out a sweater with pink pigs across the front. Mickey loved this sweater. I heard Mom going downstairs. I charged out of my room, pulling on my sweater as I ran down after her.

She was looking in her purse for her keys.

"Can I come?" I said.

"No, no, just wait here. Dad'll come home later."

"Please, let me."

"No, too much is going on. You can't go into his room."

"Please, Mom."

She walked to the front door. "Stay here," she said. "I'll be back to help you pack for your trip tomorrow. Play with Laney. I'll tell him you said hi." She opened the door and stepped out on the porch.

I followed her outside and stood on the wet lawn as she got in the car and drove off.

23

Tears filled my eyes. I walked quickly to the beach. I stumbled over the clean cold sand. I felt like I couldn't remember Mickey very well anymore. I knew he had brown eyes and freckles on his nose and his front teeth overlapped. I knew he smelled like warm flannel and he was a runt for his age and his feet turned in when he walked—but I couldn't put him all together. I'd never studied him real hard and thought, I'm going to remember this. I cried harder as I walked over the sand.

"Hallie!"

I turned. Laney was running toward me.

"What?" I screamed. When she got to me, I was bawling.

"Something happen?" she said when she saw me crying.

"They won't take me to see Mickey!" I yelled, then I crumpled down into the sand. Laney squatted down beside me. "How come?" she said gently.

"'Cause I—I acted immature when I went before." I shook with sobs. "I have to go to my aunt's tomorrow and he's going to die and I won't ever see him again." I could hear Laney start to sniffle beside me.

"What can I do?" I said, wiping my face. My cheeks burned in the cold sunlight. Laney reached under her glasses and wiped her eyes.

"Maybe you should go there by yourself," she said.

"How?"

"You could take a bus."

"By myself?"

"Yes."

"How much would it cost?" I said.

"I don't know. Go ask them."

"Yeah, I could," I said. I stood up. I could take a bus, I thought, and go up to his room and rush in before my parents could stop me, and then when they saw I could act normal, they'd let me stay.

"Do you want to come with me to the bus sta tion?" I said. "We could find out how much it costs and get a schedule."

"I have to go to church with my mom," Laney said.

"Okay. I can go by myself. Thanks . "

"Oh, wait," she said.

"What?"

"I almost forgot what I came to tell you," she said.

"What?"

"Neil, that friend of Mickey's, was looking for you just now."

"Neil Larsen?"

"Yeah, I just saw him leaving your house on his bike."

"I better catch him," I said. Laney and I walked fast back up to the street. But Neil wasn't anywhere in sight.

"I have to go," Laney said. "Are you going to go to the bus station for a schedule?"

"Yeah," I said. "I guess I'll go right now."

We said good-bye and I got my bike out of the garage. I was wishing I'd seen Neil. Mickey and Neil were best friends. And Neil liked me—I thought he had a crush on me. He'd said my hair was like angel hair and he always smiled when I came around. Seeing Neil would have been a little like seeing Mickey, I thought. I decided to ride by his house and see if he was home. It wasn't out of the way. Maybe he'd come to the bus station with me.

I turned onto the boulevard and rode past McDonald's and Dairy Queen and the high school. I turned in at the entrance to Lynnwood Acres, the housing area where Neil lived.

When I got to Neil's street, I paused at the corner. A huge Mayflower van was parked in front of his house. Its back door was open and some men were loading furniture. I remembered that Neil was moving this week.

I rode forward and stopped. Neil and his dad were talking in their front yard. Neil was wearing a blue-jean jacket and a blue cap. From a distance, he looked sort of like a little Jack Nicholson.

"Neil!" I yelled hoarsely.

He looked over and I waved. He waved at me vigorously, then said something to his dad and came running to me.

"Hi, I was looking for you," he said, smiling

"I know. My neighbor told me."

"We're moving tomorrow to Rhode Island."

"Tomorrow?"

"How's Mickey? When's he coming home?"

I couldn't just blurt out, "Neil, Mickey's dying."

"Not for a while," I said. I felt hot all of a sudden. I pulled off my parka and stuffed it in my bike basket.

"I like your pigs," Neil said.

"What?" I said, looking down at my sweater. "These?"

"Yeah." We looked at the pigs on my sweater for a moment. Then I started feeling like we were looking at my breasts, so I crossed my arms and looked at the sky.

"It's getting cloudy," I said.

"Yeah," Neil said, smiling at me.

"Do you have to help your dad or can you do something?"

"I can play awhile."

"Do they have to pack your bike?" I asked.

"No, they're going to load more stuff tomorrow. Where do you want to go?"

"Well, I have to go to the bus station for something. You want to come with me?"

"Sure," he said. He dashed over to the carport and got his bike. I waited for him, then we took off together.

As we drove through the housing development on our way to the boulevard, we talked to each other from our bikes. "Will you live near a beach in Rhode Island?" I said.

"Yeah," shouted Neil.

"That's good. Remember that day we pretended that we were riding dolphins?" I said.

Neil laughed and nodded.

"That was sort of dumb. But it was fun, wasn't it?" I yelled.

"Yeah!" he said.

"I wish we could play that game again sometime," I said.

"We can," Neil said.

"No, we can't," I said. "You're moving"—I pedaled faster and called back over my shoulder—"and Mickey's going to die!"

I stood up on my pedals and sped to the boulevard. The light at the intersection was red. I stopped and Neil pulled up close to my bike and said, "Wait!" I looked at him.

"Did you say Mickey was going to die?" he said.

I nodded.

"What's he have?"

"A tumor."

"Whew," said Neil, whistling out air. "I can't believe it. Are you sure?" Neil's eyes looked teary.

"Yeah," I said.

"Oh, that's terrible," he said. He shook his head and looked away from me.

"My parents won't let me go see him," I said. "So I have to get there by myself."

Neil turned back to me. "You should go see him," he said.

"I know. I am."

"How are you going?"

"I'm going to take a bus. That's why I'm going to the bus station. I have to get information."

The light changed. I turned onto the boulevard

and Neil followed me. We drove to the Greyhound station and parked in the parking lot. We walked inside to the information window.

"Can I have a schedule, please?" I asked the man. "Also, how much is it to Norfolk? And how long does it take to get there?"

"Costs two fifty," the man said. "Takes about forty minutes. It's twenty-five miles from here."

"Thanks." We walked back out to our bikes. I unfolded the bus schedule and looked at it. It didn't make a bit of sense to me. I handed it to Neil.

"When can I go?" I said.

Neil looked at the schedule for a minute and said, "On Sunday there are only two times: at noon and at five P.M."

"What time is it now?"

Neil cupped his hand over his digital watch. "Eleven forty-five. You could go in fifteen minutes."

"I'm not ready," I said. "I don't have any money with me. Do you?"

"No," he said. "Can you go at five?"

"Yeah, but then I'd get there when it's dark," I said. This whole plan was starting to scare me. "I think I'll go tomorrow morning. What time could I go then?"

Neil looked back at the schedule. "There's one at nine."

"What do you think I should take?" I said.

"You could pack a lunch."

"Yeah."

"You could take a book to read on the ride."

"What do you think Mickey would like?" I said.

Neil's eyes started looking teary again. He looked down at his handlebars and blinked hard for a few seconds. Then he looked back at me and said, "I don't think he needs anything. He'll probably just be glad to see you."

"Yeah."

"Yeah," Neil said, looking at me real serious. I wished he could stay with me, not have to go home or move away tomorrow. I really liked him.

"I have to go," Neil said.

"I know."

"Good luck," he said. "I hope Mickey—" He stopped.

"Have a good time in Rhode Island," I said.

Suddenly Neil got off his bike, and holding his handlebars with one hand, he leaned over and kissed me on the cheek. Then he got back on his bike and took off. When he got to the street, he waved at me. I couldn't believe him. I thought if he'd just been a little older—like eleven or twelve—I would have had a crush on him for sure.

24

Riding home, I felt nervous but happy. Tomorrow
I'll be with Mickey, I thought. I'll ride the bus to
Norfolk and stay with him in the hospital. I was sure
I could make him feel better, just by showing him
how much I loved him. Not come out and say it—
that would make him say "yuk"—but just be there
and take care of him, help him not be afraid. We
could talk about the dolphin game, pretend we were
riding them. And we could play Bosco baseball. That
was when Bosco played baseball against a team of

Mickey's socks. I could take some socks to the hospital. I burst out laughing—take some socks to the hospital! I laughed so hard, I almost ran into the curb. Take some socks! I thought that was one of the silliest things I'd thought of in a long time.

When I got to our street, I felt a raindrop hit my face. By the time I got to our garage it was raining pretty hard. I grabbed my parka and ran into the house.

I went up to my parents' room to look in Pop's desk for a map of Norfolk. I couldn't find one. I searched in all the drawers twice. I figured I'd better try to get one before Pop came home. I went downstairs and grabbed an umbrella out of the hall closet and went out the door. I walked quickly two blocks to the Exxon station on the boulevard. I tramped up to the glass door, stuck my head inside and asked the man for a map of Norfolk. He gave me one for free.

I hurried home. The car still wasn't there. Pop was taking a long time at the hospital. I went inside and spread my map out on the kitchen table and studied it for a while. I found the Norfolk bus station and the hospital on the map. They were pretty far apart, so I figured I'd have to take a taxi when I got off the bus.

The house was so quiet, I started feeling nervous. I went into the living room to wait for Pop. I turned on the TV, but I didn't pay much attention to it. Finally I decided to make a lunch to take on the trip.

It was beginning to grow dark outside as I got out a can of tuna and some bread and a jar of mayonnaise. While I was making the sandwich I picked up the kitchen phone and dialed Anne's number. She had told me to call her today. A girl answered and I asked for Anne Pine. I cradled the phone between my chin and shoulder and spread mayonnaise on my bread while I waited for Anne to come to the phone. I wondered whether or not I should tell her about my trip to Norfolk. I thought part of her would understand, but the other part wouldn't. I opened the can of tuna.

"Hello?"

"Anne!"

"No, this is her roommate, Betsy. Who's this?"

"Her sister," I said. "Is Anne there?"

"No, she left over an hour ago."

"She did?"

"She caught a three-thirty plane out of Raleigh."

"For where?" I asked in a small voice.

"Norfolk. Your dad's picking her up, right?"

"When did she decide to go to Norfolk?"

"When your dad called a few hours ago."

"Thanks." I hung up.

Anne was in Norfolk? Mom and Pop and Mickey and Anne were all together in Norfolk? My whole family was there—except me! I picked up my half made tuna sandwich and hurled it across the room. I knocked over a kitchen chair and another one. I was closest to Mickey of anybody! Why wasn't I with them? I was eleven years old, dammit—not a baby, not a stupid idiot who couldn't visit a sick person! "Damn! Hell!" I yelled. I grabbed some silverware from the sink and threw it on the floor. I slammed my hand against the refrigerator, then ripped some magnetic potholders off the door and threw them across the room.

Suddenly I heard loud knocking at the front door. I stumbled to the door and threw it open. Mrs. Bankly and Laney were standing on the porch.

"Darling, your father called and asked me to bring you over to our house."

"Why?"

"He said he'd call you at our house and talk to you there. He doesn't want you to be alone."

"I'll be there in a minute. I'll be right over."

Mrs. Bankly stood there like she was waiting for me. "You can go," I said to her as I started to close the door.

"I'd better wait for you," she said.

"Mom, I'll wait for her," Laney said. "Go back home."

"Well, all right," Mrs. Bankly said. And she walked across our porch and down the stairs.

I stepped back from the door and Laney came in.

"Something's happened," I said. "My sister—my sister's in Norfolk and—"

"I know," Laney said. "My mom said your dad sounded really upset."

"I better go now," I said. I started shaking all over and looking at her. I needed her help. I couldn't move.

"Get your coat," she said, giving me a gentle push.

I could hardly feel my legs underneath me as I ran up the stairs. I got my parka out of my room and pulled it on as I came downstairs.

"Oh, I need money," I said. I ran back upstairs and got birthday money out of my top dresser drawer. I ran back down to Laney.

"Take your bike to the bus station," she said.

"I know." I opened the door.

"Do you have everything?" she said.

"Yes."

"Then go, as fast as you can!"

Suddenly I remembered Mickey saying that old rhyme: "Run, run, as fast as you can! You can't catch me, I'm the Gingerbread Man!" It made me unbearably sad.

"I'm going," I said. I ran out the door and off the porch. I grabbed my bike out of the garage and took off in the rain.

25

The tires of my bike seemed to slash the pavement as they whished through the rain. I didn't shake or cry. I stood up on my pedals and drove to the boulevard. I felt wild but totally concentrated. I sped past Kentucky Fried Chicken, McDonald's, Dairy Queen. I drove to the door of the Greyhound station, kicked down my kickstand, and tore inside.

"Could I please have a ticket for the five o'clock bus to Norfolk?" I asked the man behind the counter. I was dripping with rain.

"Nope—you just missed the five."

Damn! I couldn't believe it. "If my mother drives me there, which road should she take?" I said.

"Route Sixty-five."

"How does she get there?"

"Tell her to turn left onto the boulevard. Ride till she sees signs for Sixty-five West."

"Then what does she do to get to Norfolk?"

He sighed. "Get on Sixty-five till Exit Nine. Then follow the signs."

I turned and ran out the door. I jumped on my bike, lowered my head against the rain, and pedaled out of the parking lot. I turned onto the boulevard and zoomed north with the traffic. I rode close to the edge of the highway and followed the signs to Route 65. The rain was beating my head, my face, my hands, and my knees. Cars sped past me, spraying water over my shoes and tires, almost blowing me off the road. But I felt like I was made of iron and steel. I was a steely machine and my bursting heart was my engine.

I rode for miles through the rain on 65. I wasn't afraid of getting lost or being hit by a car. I didn't even feel very tired. If my bike had broken, I would have left it beside the road and run the rest of the way. I pedaled past drive-ins, restaurants, motels, past deserted stretches of highway with only trees and fields and ocean air. Once I saw the lights of a house in the distance and I wished I was safe inside it with my family. But I didn't think that for long. Darkness kept rising in me, filling my rainy heart, breaking it over and over again, and each break made me pedal faster and harder. Sometimes I thought I saw monsters riding by—headless men and ghosts on bikes—and I saw my whole family shattered and sort of scattered across the sky like pieces of a burnt-out firecracker. I felt alone, like I knew nobody on the whole planet and even the cars passing by me were in another world. Once a shrill sad scream filled my ears, and I don't know if it came from me or from a dream in my head, but I felt like my whole body was turning inside out. I held tight to the handlebars and pushed my feet against the pedals, and my legs kept pumping, and I rushed through waves of horrible dreams, through the wind and the rain, pumping my pedals like I was grinding the darkness.

I felt like I'd been riding for years when I saw signs for Norfolk. I pedaled off Route 65 onto Exit 9. I was shaking uncontrollably, and my thoughts had no beginning and no end. Something made me make the right turns until finally I found myself downtown. I saw signs for Robert E. Lee Memorial and I followed them until I came to the hospital grounds. I rode to the pediatrics entrance. I jumped off my bike, tripped over the curb, and fell down on the pavement. I picked myself up and limped into the waiting room.

A nurse was sitting at the reception desk. She was looking down at some papers. A security guard was talking to her. I ran down the hall to the elevator.

"Wait!" I heard behind me as I scooted into the empty car. I pushed 4, and the doors closed as I heard footsteps coming down the hall. I went up.

I was shaking and my teeth were chattering, but still I felt like I was made of steel. I got off on the fourth floor and no one was at the reception desk. Everything was quiet. I looked down the hall. There at the end was my mother in Pop's arms. Anne was sitting on a bench with her head in her hands, and two doctors were with them.

My eyes darted to the room I knew was Mickey's. No one was looking my way, so I charged down the hall to Mickey's door, opened it, and slipped in. I don't know what I expected to see—Mickey reading a Hardy Boys book; Mickey craning his neck to see me; or Mickey lying there with tubes and machines going in and out of him. I don't know what I expected, but when I looked at his bed, I just saw old Mickey lying there very very still. No books, no tubes, just his frail, unmoving self.

I said, "Squirt blossom, I'm here," but as soon as I said it I felt funny.

"Mickey," I said softly, and I moved closer to his bed. I stared at his face. It was pale as a pearl and his eyes were closed. My heart was still. I didn't shake or cry. My only problem was I didn't know what to say —because Mickey wasn't there. I knew it for sure. His body was lying there, but he was gone. It was like the time I'd seen a stray yellow cat in our backyard and later that same day I saw it dead in the middle of the road and when I picked it up to move it, I knew it wasn't there anymore. It was like I was holding a cat suit and the cat had slipped out. In that same way, I knew Mickey was gone.

But I wanted to talk to him. I kept looking at him. I stepped closer to his bed and touched his sheet. I said, "I came to take care of you." In a low, whispery voice, I said, "I came to play with you." Rain dripped from me onto the bed and floor. "I thought we could pretend that—that you're riding a dolphin, not pretending on the sand, but really riding one, riding it way out in the ocean. You can, you know. . . ." I touched his hair. I ran my finger down over his cold forehead, his freckled nose, his mouth, and his chin. I lifted his hand and watched it drop back onto the bed.

"Deader'n a doornail," I said. It was a weird thing to say. And what's worse is I laughed after I said it. I laughed even though I loved Mickey more than anything else in the world and he'd just gone away. I turned his face toward me and said, "'Bye. I love you." Then I pressed my lips to his cheek and laughed very softly.

To this day I worry that maybe I wasn't reverent enough, maybe I should have acted more serious when I was alone with Mickey's body. But I felt like he was alive—that he just wasn't in that body in that bed—and I thought it was funny he'd slipped out like that and left all of us behind. But now I can hardly admit that I stood there laughing and talking like I did. I tell myself it must have been the wind on my ride whipping my brains that made me behave that way.

I acted more normal when I left his room and limped down the long hall to my family. Pop saw me first and said, "What the hell?" Then Anne said, "Hallie!" And my mother let out a little cry and grabbed me. I started to cry. I sobbed that I'd ridden my bike there. Pop asked one of the doctors to please look me over, so she took me into a little room and put me on a bed and helped me take off my clothes. She checked my heart and blood pressure. Pop came in while I was sitting there and said, "Hallie, your brother passed away." I put my arms around his neck and cried into his collar.

26

It was almost midnight when we left the hospital. Pop put my bike in the trunk of the car and I sat in the backseat with Anne.

At home, I got in my bed and stayed there for a few days. I had a fever and my limbs were exhausted from my bike trip. Pop and Anne sat with me a lot; so did Laney and my Aunt Mary and Uncle Bert, who flew in from Daytona Beach. Everyone tried to comfort my mother. She stayed in her room by herself most of the time. But the afternoon after

Mickey's funeral, she came into my room. She sat on the edge of my bed and touched my hair. She said, "Dolly?"

"What?" I said.

She looked at me silently for a few seconds. Then she said softly, "This is a hard time." She pulled on my curls and said, "Your hair's too long."

"I want to let it grow out," I said. She patted my hair, looking far away.

"Do you know where I can get my hair straightened?" I said.

She said I shouldn't get my hair straightened, that most people would give their right arm to have hair like mine. I argued with her a little. It was a way to get her to talk to me. Actually I was starting to like my hair.

She stayed with me, and we talked for almost an hour. She acted surprised when I told her that Laney read really hard books. She said, "Okay," when I told her I wanted a bra with a little padding in it. She laughed when I told her I wanted to gain weight in my thighs. Before she left me, she gave me a long kiss on my forehead. The spot her lips touched felt warm and glowing.

I sat up and looked out the window. The sun had gone down. The sky was gray except for a few streaks of light. I felt very peaceful. I knew Mickey was okay somewhere without me. Now I just had to be okay without him. I wanted to remember this feeling. I watched some sea gulls swoop up over the sea grass, then fly away into the soft, silver light.

MARY POPE OSBORNE is a first-rate storyteller and the author of numerous works of fiction and nonfiction for all ages Her books for Random House include *Many Religions, One World* and the *Magic Tree House* series. *Run, Run, As Fast as You Can* was her first novel.

Ms. Osborne and her husband, Will, divide their time between New York City and Bucks County, Pennsylvania.